SEEKING JUSTICE

A TUCKER ASHLEY WESTERN ADVENTURE

SEEKING JUSTICE

C. M. WENDELBOE

FIVE STAR
A part of Gale, a Cengage Company

Farmington Hills, Mich • San Francisco • New York • Waterville, Maine
Meriden, Conn • Mason, Ohio • Chicago

LIBRARY OF CONGRESS CATALOGING-IN-PUBLICATION DATA

Names: Wendelboe, C. M., author.
Title: Seeking justice / C. M. Wendelboe.
Description: Waterville, Maine : Five Star Publishing, a part of Cengage Learning, Inc., [2018] | Series: A Tucker Ashley western adventure
Identifiers: LCCN 2018013040 | ISBN 9781432845964 (hardcover) | ISBN 9781432845971 (ebook) | ISBN 9781432845988 (ebook)
Subjects: LCSH: Frontier and pioneer life—Fiction. | Outlaws—Fiction. | GSAFD: Western stories.
Classification: LCC PS3623.E53 S44 2018 | DDC 813/.6—dc23 LC record available at https://lccn.loc.gov/2018013040

First Edition. First Printing: September 2018
Find us on Facebook—https://www.facebook.com/FiveStarCengage
Visit our website—http://www.gale.cengage.com/fivestar/
Contact Five Star Publishing at FiveStar@cengage.com

Printed in Mexico
1 2 3 4 5 6 7 22 21 20 19 18

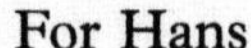

For Hans

ACKNOWLEDGMENTS

For my editors Alice Duncan, Erin Bealmear, Cathy Kulka, and Tiffany Schofield, who continue to be supportive and keep my nose to the literary whetstone; to the South Dakota Historical Society for valuable research background information in preparation for this novel; and for my wife, Heather, webmaster, photographer, and first critic, who continues to be bossy when it comes to my writing. Thank goodness.

CHAPTER 1

Tucker Ashley grabbed the side of the canned-goods shelf to keep from falling when Wilson Dawes hit the ladder with the door. The deputy marshal stumbled over the threshold and bumped his head on the door jamb overhead as he stormed into Moore Mercantile.

"I need you, Tucker," Will sputtered. Frozen sweat stuck to his florid face as he gazed up the ladder like a youngster asking his father for help. Even though Will was as old as Tucker, the marshal always looked like he was a lost child. Perhaps it was because he dressed like he was going to church, or the way he maintained perfect politeness when he was in public.

"There goes that pretty deputy marshal" Tucker heard more than one woman breathe as Will strolled by on the sidewalk. This morning, his coiffured looks were the farthest thing from his mind.

Tucker glanced down while he continued stocking shelves. "Can't you see I'm busy putting these cans of peaches away? And wipe your damned boots. I'm the one who's got to clean up after you."

Will's jingle bobs tinkled against his Spanish rowels as he knocked the snow and frozen dirt from his knee-highs so polished, a man could shave in them.

"Now what's so important you got to bust in here and—"

"There's been a murder at the Bucket of Blood." Will took his silk bandana from around his neck and dabbed sweat off his face, despite the chilling temperatures.

"Born in a barn?" Tucker said. "Close the door—you're letting the cold in."

Will glanced nervously up the street toward the saloon before shutting the door. He wiped frost off the window pane and peered out a last time before backing up to the stove in the middle of the floor.

Tucker stepped down from the ladder. He took off his apron and draped it over his shoulder. "Now what's a murder got to do with me?"

"Harmy's been killed," Will said. "And a roustabout off the steamer, too."

"Old Harmy," Tucker breathed. He dried his hands on his flour sack apron before grabbing a cracker from a tin warming atop the stove. "Who'd ever want to hurt him?" Harmy operated the Bucket of Blood like an orphanage for wayward and soiled doves. The girls who worked the cribs upstairs thought of Harmy more like a father or uncle than the owner of the only saloon in town. He gave them a place to sleep and three squares a day. And if they got the itch, Harmy provided them with medicine to cure it. "How did it happen?"

"Makes no difference how it happened." Lorna Moore emerged from the back room balancing a bolt of calico cloth in her arms. Her dark eyes seemed to bore a hole into Tucker before she turned her wrath on Will. "What happens at the Bucket of Blood—or any other unsavory place in Ft. Pierre—is no concern of Tucker's." She craned her neck up to look Tucker in the eye. "Or did you forget your promise."

"I didn't forget." Tucker sighed. Since rescuing Lorna from the renegade Lakota Blue Boy, Tucker had promised her he would settle down. Become a shopkeeper in her store. Live the quiet life while he started a family. Yet even though their marriage was only weeks away, his heart pumped faster at the mere mention of a murder in town. And at the thought of escaping the confines of the mercantile for one last *hooraw* before Lorna domesticated him.

Tucker poured Will a cup of coffee and put the pot back atop the stove. He wrapped his trembling hands around the hot mug, and Tucker nodded to the door. "But it won't take Will long to tell me," he said to Lorna. "I'll be right back." He grabbed his own cup and followed Will outside.

"Don't you get any fool notions about getting involved," Lorna called to Tucker as he closed the door.

Outside, the wind had picked up since Tucker had walked to the general store this morning, and he chin-pointed to a bench in front of the mercantile. "You better sit down before you fall," he told Will.

Will walked on shaky legs to the bench. He brushed snow off the plank of wood and plopped down. He held the hot cup close to him as he looked down the street to the saloon where a crowd gathered. Men huddled together in front of the Bucket as if they were afraid to enter and see the murder scene for themselves, yet wanting to be the first there if the saloon keeper rose from the dead.

"That John Kane blocking the door?" Tucker asked. A man as wide as he was tall filled the doorway. A cowboy tried walking around him, but the blacksmith tossed him aside like he was tossing aside a sack of feed.

"That's John. He was upstairs—"

"Spending his money with one of the ladies?" Tucker groaned. John had been a blacksmith all his life, concerned with hard work and bragging that he had no interest in womenfolk. That was, until Harmy introduced John to one of the ladies with a particular fondness for fat men with fatter pocketbooks.

"John was upstairs when the shooting happened. He's the one who found Harmy and the roustabout," Will said. "Was hard on him, too, him being bestest friends with Harmy."

"Now tell me what happened down there."

Will spilled coffee on his wispy, blond mustache and down onto his marshal's star pinned to his chest. He swiped a coat sleeve across his face but left the star tarnished. "Four men entered the Bucket this morning," he began. "They knew there would be no one in the saloon at that time of day. They beat old Harmy until he told them the combination to his floor safe. And when he gave them the number and they had his money, they still beat him so bad he died right there."

"And you say there was no one else in the saloon at the time?"

Will shook his head. "Empty except for Harmy. All the girls were still sleeping in their cribs."

"Then how do you know what happened?"

"That roustabout." Will nodded to a steamer moored at the loading dock on this side of the Missouri. "He passed out last night, and Harmy just let him sleep it off on the floor under the faro table in back. When he come to, he seen everything."

Tucker sat beside Will. "You're not making any sense. I thought you said the killers shot this roustabout?"

Will finished his coffee and set the cup on the wooden walkway. He blew into his hands, ignoring the frozen snot on his upper lip. "They left him for dead, but he wasn't. He managed to tell me what went down before he went under. I sent for the army doctor at Ft. Sully, but he ain't come yet. A couple of Harmy's girls are keeping the man comfortable until the sawbones arrives."

Tucker stretched out his legs and looked at the saloon. The crowd had become louder, savage intentions sounding in their voices, which rose and fell with the biting wind. Before long, they would work up enough courage to go after the killers. Shootings and an occasional knifing had been a near-daily occurrence at the Bucket of Blood since Harmy opened it, catering to the trapper that happened by, or the freighter off a boat, or the roustabout or teamster wanting to boil off a little steam. But Harmy's death took violence to a new level—he was universally liked, as much for the girls he rescued as for the hand-up he'd give any man in need. "You still never explained what I have to do with Harmy's death."

"I need to form a posse."

"And you want me along?"

Will picked the frozen snot from his mustache. "I need a tracker."

Tucker pointed to the crowd. "There's bound to be any number of men capable of following the killers' tracks. Especially in this snow."

"But you've been on a posse before. I never was."

Tucker laughed. "Well, you wanted the job. Maybe you should have told the territorial marshal to make you a turnkey or something instead." After Tucker had killed the last crooked Dakota territorial deputy marshal in a gunfight, he'd kicked around the notion of taking the deputy job himself. But Wilson Dawes had pestered his brother-in-law—Dakota territorial marshal out of Yankton—for the job. He'd appointed Will the deputy marshal and exiled him to the upper Missouri. Will assumed the role: tall and fit and powerfully built, with a look he bragged was akin to that of Colonel Custer. Will walked the streets of Ft. Pierre, tipping his hat to ladies on his way to lunch with a local businessman. Or giving lectures at the Methodist Church on the virtues of abstaining from alcohol. Which he always did.

Now, confronted with something many frontier lawmen faced—forming a posse to pursue murderers—he floundered, not knowing how to go about asking men for help. Or what to expect. "Those men down there is a mob," Will said. "I'm sure one or two would be passable trackers. But as a mob, they'd destroy more sign than they found when they go after the killers."

Will was right. In another hour—two at most—the mob would grow enough liquid courage to set off after the gang. And wipe out any hope of a true man tracker following them. "Who did the roustabout say killed Harmy and shot him?"

"The guy never seen them before." Will stood and began to pace the frozen ground in front of the mercantile. He looked at his reflection in the glass and patted his hair down. "But one was a kid. Just a runt." He stomped his feet to get his circulation going. " 'Bout twenty years old, he said. And another guy not much bigger, but a heap older. Some farmer who kept lookout at the door—"

"How'd he know it was a farmer?"

"He wore bib overalls," Will answered. "Who but a farmer wears bibs?"

"I think I saw him," Tucker said. "He wandered into the store this morning. I paid him no mind. I was up the ladder when he came in asking for candy. Lorna wrapped some licorice sticks up in a newspaper, and the man left. I couldn't tell you what he looked like except he had a thick accent—Swede or Norwegian. Hard to tell; there's so many of them hereabouts."

"Maybe he wasn't the gang's lookout."

"He was the lookout, all right," Tucker said. He downed the last of the coffee and tossed the grounds into the snow. "What did the last man look like?"

"That roustabout started shaking real bad when he told me." Will himself began to tremble, and he grabbed the store front for support. "He was a big guy. Leader, as he was giving the orders. But not as big as us—five or six inches shorter," Will said. "Five-ten, five-eleven maybe. And husky. Like he'd done hard work all his life."

"That fits a lot of fellers in these parts." Tucker shrugged.

"Most any farmer from up north, and most cow hands hereabouts, have been filled out from years of busting their tails."

"But one with a chunk of ear missing, and a scar that runs down the side of his neck?"

Tucker closed his eyes and envisioned the Wanted posters he'd seen. "Did he have a southern accent?"

"The roustabout said he could hardly tell what the man said, his drawl was so thick."

Tucker had looked at enough Wanted posters these last years, when he scouted for the army, posters that proclaimed the U.S. government still wanted certain Confederate war criminals. If their crimes were bad enough.

And by the description Will gave, his crimes were—if it was Justice Cauther. Justice had been a cross-border raider, captured when some Union soldier trailed Justice to a Kansas saloon, and he'd been captured when he passed out drunk. After the war and after escaping the Union POW camp in New York, Justice took up where he left off. The Cauther gang had terrorized folks—and lawmen—in the territory for years. Tucker had no desire to go after them. He had done enough of that during the war. Besides, it just wasn't any of his business. "You don't need me to find it." He picked up Will's coffee cup and started for the store. "Get one of those men down there. Even *you* could track the gang in this fresh snow. Or follow the trail of deaths they're bound to leave."

"But you could follow them through hell," Will pleaded. "You can track anything."

Tucker rubbed his temple to ease his headache. Tracking—finding men who didn't want to be found—was the one skill his father had taught him. Tracking game in the woods of Pennsylvania had been like a fun puzzle, working out direction, aging the tracks to figure out when the deer or the fox made them.

But tracking Confederate soldiers during the war had been serious business, and he had garnered a reputation as the Union's premier tracker. More times than he wanted to remember, he had trailed some Confederate wanted badly by the Union, only to be pulled off while the regular troops swooped in for the kill or capture. He had proved himself just too invaluable to the North for them to risk his being killed.

After the war, his skills had served him well when the army of the frontier needed man trackers to find elusive Indians. Up until he quit to build a life with Lorna. "I can't help you," he said as he turned to leave.

"They abducted Velma on their way out of the saloon," Will called after him.

Tucker stopped mid-stride. "Jack's Velma?"

"The same."

Velma had drifted into Ft. Pierre with a pretty face and a smile and little else. She had been brought out in one of those heart and hand clubs matching bachelors with eligible women. Only her match had been killed in a knife fight the day before she stepped off the boat. So she had done the only thing she could do in the river town—entertain men. Harmy had set her up in a crib with the other girls above the saloon, and she had been one of the popular doves. With flowing, curly, blond hair and bright-green eyes, she bragged she could charm the pants right off most any man. She had spent the last eight months proving that.

And she was the only girl Tucker's friend, Jack Worman, had ever loved.

Jack often said that—as soon as he saved enough from his army scout pay—he and Velma planned to get married. Build a family on a homestead they had picked out down-river. Except now she'd been taken, and Jack was scouting with the army somewhere out west. Tucker owed his friend far more than rescuing his girl. He owed Jack his life on more than one occasion. "Go to the livery and get my mule saddled," Tucker told Will. "Bring him to the jail, and I'll meet you there."

Will shook Tucker's hand like he was pumping a jack handle. "I will, soon's I get the rest of my posse rounded up."

Tucker was bent over rummaging through his foot locker when Lorna burst into the room. Her eyes narrowed and her face flushed crimson when she saw Tucker's gun belt slung over his shoulder. "Just what are you doing?"

Tucker stuffed two boxes of pistol ammunition into his saddlebags and grabbed his Sharps rifle from behind the door. "Marshal Dawes needs someone to track those men who killed Harmy and that roustabout."

"But you promised." Lorna stood with her hands on her hips, blocking the door. "Daddy's fixing to catch the boat at Yankton next week before the river freezes over. You're supposed to meet him before the wedding." She waved her hand at his weapons. "And now you want to go gallivanting across the country? You won't be back before Daddy arrives." Old Man Moore—as his business rivals had called him for decades—planned to be at his mercantile store on the Upper Missouri by next week to meet his future son-in-law and give away his only daughter.

Tucker slipped on his sheepskin coat and strapped his gun belt around his waist before he stepped around Lorna. "If it was just Marshal Dawes wanting me to ride to catch those killers, I would tell him do it without my help. But they took Velma."

"That whore from the saloon?"

"Velma's a human being," Tucker faced Lorna. "And she's Jack Worman's woman."

"At least he'll have a woman."

"What's that supposed to mean?" Tucker asked.

"Not to be surprised when you come back and I'm not here."

Chapter 2

Justice Cauther reined his dappled-gray gelding atop a high hill overlooking the river town two miles to the east. He squinted to see smoke rising from chimneys and the pilot tower of a river boat just above the horizon. No one followed them. But then, he hadn't expected anyone to be up at that hour. The town was as dead at dawn as that old saloon keeper and that roostered-up roustabout who crawled from under a back table.

He closed his spyglass—compliments of a Dutch trader captain he'd killed just off the coast of Taiwan five years ago—and stored it back in his saddlebags. "I need a cup of tea," he announced as he dismounted. "And y'all might want coffee."

Since Justice sailed merchant ships after he'd escaped a Union POW camp, he'd witnessed the benefits of tea. When many men—especially in the west—suffered dysentery and other stomach ails that would kill or cripple a strong man, the Chinese had no such problems. Cauther didn't especially like tea, but he'd learned that boiling water for tea killed all sorts of gut critters that could sideline a man. He'd never visited an opium den yet where the Chinamen had stomach ailments.

He climbed down from his horse and tied him to a tree stump in the middle of tall prairie grass.

"I got the pots," Elias said as he rooted in his bags for two tin pots. He hitched his bib overalls up while he squatted beside firewood he'd gathered. He set the pots on top of rocks he'd arranged around the wood and reached into his pocket for a match.

Justice fished tea out of a canvas bag, and coffee grounds from another as he watched their back trail. Before he died, the saloonkeeper told him the county sheriff went to Sioux City for a funeral, leaving a deputy U.S. marshal who couldn't shoot his way out of a knife fight to guard the town. Still, Justice hadn't lived and terrorized folks as long as he had without being cautious. And always in the back of his mind was the haunting thought of Tucker Ashley living in Ft. Pierre. When he'd heard that Ashley was in town, Justice had mixed feelings—part of him wanted to wait outside the mercantile and kill him when he left for the day. But Justice's love of money won over his passion for revenge, and he just wanted to ride as far away as possible.

He waited until the water was hot before sprinkling just the right amount of grounds and crushed tea leaves into the tin pots. Soon, the odor wafted past his nose. *Damn, I make a good cup of good coffee.* It was the one thing he insisted on doing on the trail: making coffee for the others while his tea steeped.

Velma burst out in fresh wails. Tears mixed with black kohl froze to her cheeks, and one eye had started to swell where Henny had got a little too rough with her. She struggled against the rope securing her hands, and she nearly fell before grabbing on to the saddle horn. "Can't you shut her up?" Justice said. "That whining is getting to me."

Henny Cauther—Justice's younger half-brother—shoved Velma from the saddle as she sat in front of him. She fell to the ground and landed on top of sharp rocks. Blood dripped from deep scrapes on her arms, and Henny burst out laughing. He hopped down from his bay, compliments of a U.S. Army trooper he had ambushed this spring outside Lincoln. "I'll do what I can to keep her quiet." He wrapped his hand around Velma's matted blond hair and dragged her over a rise. The last thing Justice saw before they disappeared over the hill was Henny stuffing a snotty bandana in her mouth and loosening his gun belt.

Elias Gates drew his coat tight around his bib overalls. He bent to the ground and added wood to the fire. "Ve should haf' left her in the saloon," he said in his thick Norwegian accent. "Damn whore's gonna' slow us down."

Justice blew air into his cupped hands and sat on a rock beside Elias. "Henny wanted the girl," he said flatly.

Elias nudged the pile of wood with his boot. "So now your pimply faced brother calls the shots for the Cauther gang?"

Justice bent over and blew on the struggling flames until they flared up again. "You know how the kid is with women." Justice rubbed his hands over the heat. "Give him a couple years and it'll be out of his system."

"Ve might not haf a couple years if a posse picks up our trail."

Justice motioned to a rider slowly approaching the camp from the direction of town. "Relax. Between me hiding our tracks and Gall watching our back trail, it's not likely we'll be followed. Besides, the whore was a witness. We couldn't leave her."

"And we *never* leave witnesses," Gall Manahan said. He rode into camp and dismounted. He carefully and lovingly slipped his English Whitworth target rifle into his scabbard that hung from the side of his saddle, a gift for killing Union general Labor at Gettysburg. Gall—small and wiry as any Indian—looked even smaller next to his rifle. "And the whore got a look at *all* of us."

"She vill still slow us down," Elias repeated. "And that bawling—"

"Relax." Justice grabbed the tea pot from the fire and filled his cup. "By the time Henny gets through with her," he grinned, "the woman will be too exhausted to cry out."

Elias looked in the direction Henny and Velma had disappeared, her cries bouncing off the surrounding hills but becoming less pronounced, as if she was becoming exhausted. "I'm just worried about a posse. Ve haf been lucky so far, but—"

"Luck's got nothing to do with it," Gall said. "We've eluded every posse sent after us because Justice made it happen."

Justice tipped the brim of his Stetson. "Thanks for noticing." He approached Elias, the closest thing in this life he had to a friend. He'd met Elias while they were both imprisoned at Elmira, the Union prisoner-of-war camp in New York the southern prisoners termed "Hellmira" for the brutal conditions. Elmira offered great opportunities for people like Elias, however. He stole food from fellow starving prisoners too injured or too sick with fever to object and shoved the same prisoners aside when fresh water was passed around. Justice had sat back and watched the Norseman from Minnesota—who'd signed up to fight for the south—make his rounds of the camp at night. More than a few Confederate soldiers died of exposure when someone stole their blankets during the night, while Elias never went cold.

But he'd always been a worrier. Justice slapped him on the back. "When has any posse ever been able to follow us?"

Elias looked toward Ft. Pierre. They were miles from the river town with no one on their trail. "But ve never had to worry about Tucker Ashley tracking for the law. You know what trouble he can be—"

"I thought you said he was not going to be a problem," Justice snapped.

"Yeah," Gall said, "I thought you said he was strapped to that mercantile job?" He squatted beside the fire and poured himself a cup of coffee. He wrapped his hands around the hot tin cup and looked up at Elias. "We wouldn't have chanced robbing that saloon keeper without your assurance about Ashley."

Elias rubbed his forehead. "I saw him stocking shelves. He looked real natural with that apron around him. Like he vas born to it. But if he gets a notion to throw in with the law—"

"Then we'll deal with him." Justice handed Elias a cup of coffee. "Take it easy. I've been doubly careful hiding our trail. Even if he decides to toss his apron aside and join a posse, he won't be able to find us." They had ridden fast away from the river town, Justice picking spots to ride where the snow had blown clear, skirting clumps of the grass high enough to hide a man and a horse; making certain no one could work out their trail. Still . . .

Justice looked back toward the river and shielded his hand over his teacup as snow swirled around him. When they had learned the saloonkeeper kept money in a safe in the floor, Justice thought it would be an easy job. Until he found out Tucker Ashley lived in the river town, and Justice put the job on hold until he could be assured Ashley wouldn't be a factor. Ashley's abilities as a man tracker were told around campfires at night. He used his skills to scout for the army, and at times to ride with posses hunting owlhoots. If Justice believed half the tales about Ashley, he might even be *his* equal in deciphering a trail.

So Justice sent Elias—plain and looking like any other farmer struggling along the Missouri—into the mercantile to get a feel for Ashley. When Elias returned, he explained that Ashley was browbeaten by his woman, who ran the store. She had plans for him other than traipsing across the prairie after a bunch of killers.

Justice feared no man, but if Ashley took to tracking them after the robbery, that would complicate things for them. And all he wanted was one more big job to send them on their way to warmer climes. *Or, I might take the fight to Ashley if he follows us,* Justice thought.

I would kill Ashley in a heartbeat, if we had time. But right now the last person I want on our ass is him.

Chapter 3

When Will stepped down from his Appaloosa, he twisted his ankle on a rock. His leg buckled, and he grabbed fast to the cantle of his tooled saddle. He recovered his balance and hobbled to where Tucker bent over, studying the ground. "You lost their trail," Will said. "I thought you were the best the army has."

Tucker didn't look up, but kept his face lowered, staring into the sun to spot hoof prints. Tracks invisible to the eye almost always stood out in contrast when one looked at them with the sun at your face, and he squinted to pick up anomalies on the frozen ground. "Best the army *had.*"

Tucker finally spotted a hoof scuff, then another, leading west toward a butte where the faint tracks headed. He thought the butte was a mile away, but it was hard to tell—places had a way of fooling a man in the tall-grass prairie. "The men we're following are not your average men," he said. "But you already knew that."

"What's that supposed to mean?"

"We'll talk about it later. We might as well take a break." Tucker pointed to the mile of flat prairie leading up to the tall butte. "When we start across that flat, we'll be out in the open, and we'd better not stop until we get across. A short rest won't hurt us none if we suddenly have to make a dash across open ground."

Marshal Dawes laughed. "I doubt the killers will be wasting

time sitting around in the cold waiting for us. They'll want to be out of the territory as quickly as possible."

"You sound as if you'd just as soon *not* catch up with them. Like you might be a little afraid, Will."

"That's nonsense." Will nodded to the others following slowly along a deep deer trail. "Way I figure it, we'll be a match for them whenever we run them to ground." He ran his fingers through his flowing, sandy hair. *Damned pretty man,* Tucker thought.

"Like I said, these aren't your normal men we're after." Tucker looked past Will at the others coming up the trail. "A rest?"

"Take a few," Will called out. He turned to his posse and watched them dismount.

John Kane—the fat blacksmith who had been Harmy's closest friend and the first to volunteer to hunt the killers—stepped down from his mare, Sadie. He untied the strap on his saddlebag and grabbed his coffee pot before turning to Ronnie Barnes. "Rustle up some firewood."

"Rustle some up yourself."

"Not much of a trail rider, are you?"

Ronnie stepped toward John. "What you mean by that, old man?"

Bowlegged Frank North stepped between John and Ronnie, who was acting like a banty rooster. "John didn't mean nothing by it," Frank said, tossing his pillow aside. The bowlegged man had been a cowboy nearly as long as Tucker had been alive, coming up north on the Goodnight-Loving Trail in 1860 and staying in the North Country working spreads. He was experienced on the trail, but his hemorrhoids killed him sitting a saddle. He wouldn't have been able to ride across the street if he didn't put the pillow between the saddle and his bony butt. "Leave him be."

Ronnie pointed to John. "He sounds like the foreman what put the run on us."

"Don't take it out on John," Tucker said. "He didn't fire you." Ronnie and Frank North had had more than a casual run-in with the foreman of the Rocking H—they'd been run off the ranch during the past summer, when ranch hands caught Ronnie and Frank trailing five calves with questionable brands. And it helped them none when the foreman found a running iron in Ronnie's saddlebag. They'd both been lucky to have gotten away with their skins. Will had been called, but there was not enough evidence to arrest them. Or hang them, though the Rocking H hands were eager to stretch the pair's necks from a stout piece of hemp rope.

Tucker drew Will away from the others gathering around the fire. "Is that the best you can come up with for a posse? You know as well as I do those two were guilty as sin."

Will looked past Tucker. Frank had ushered Ronnie aside, and the two argued between themselves. "I had to get *somebody.* All I could offer was a dollar a day, and those two were still out of work, riding the grub line since that incident at the Rocking H. Besides, there was no evidence they stole those cattle."

"Then what about him?" Tucker motioned to Pasqual Lemieux. Lemieux lazily picked up wood for the fire, whistling as if he had all day to build some heat.

"He was like John," Will said. "He demanded to come along. The gang snatched his gambling money off the table when he was visiting the outhouse in back of the Bucket of Blood. By the time he responded to the shot that killed the roustabout and stumbled into the saloon holding his trousers up, the gang had fled. 'I'll be damned if I'll let those bastards get away with my winnings,' he told me."

"And what about that crowd in front of the saloon screaming for blood? Don't tell me there wasn't a man there who would ride a posse with you."

"There wasn't a *sober* man who would ride," Will answered. "Last thing I need is drunks on the trail of . . . killers."

Will took his hatred for the bottle too far. Tucker would have preferred drunks who could actually ride and shoot than the bunch Will had scrounged together.

The coffee pot shook as the water heated, and Tucker poured a cup. He motioned for Will to follow him away from ears of the rest crowding around the flames. "Your posse consists of a blacksmith too fat to bend over, two cowboys who were all but strung up for rustling, and a gambler who's only packing little guns in a shoulder rig. And a deputy marshal on his first track of the most ruthless bunch in the territory. When they find out we're trailing the Cauthers—"

"Shush!" Will turned his back and lowered his voice. "Who says it's the Cauthers?"

"I heard how that dying roustabout described the killers. And this." Tucker bent and carefully brushed snow from the hard ground, revealing a partial hoof print. "Way I've heard it, no one hides their trail like Justice Cauther." He stood and looked to the butte. "When *were* you going to tell the others?"

Will kicked a clod of dirt with the toe of his boot. "Do you think I'd get anyone to ride along if I told them we were going after the Cauthers? Maybe John, as Harmy was his best friend. But the rest wouldn't be that . . . foolish."

"You mean because Harmy always set aside the prettiest girl when John visited the Bucket?"

"That, too," Will said. "Point is, I needed a posse. And being honest wouldn't get me any men."

"Nobody ever accused you of being honest."

"Thanks," Will said. "I think."

Tucker shook his head as he looked at Will's crack posse. John had stoked the fire like he did in his blacksmith shop—

high and hot enough that the Cauthers could have seen and smelled it for miles. Ronnie still cursed loud enough that the same people could hear him a mile away, and Frank carefully laid his pillow on a rock before gingerly setting down. And sometime during the last few minutes, Pasqual had burned himself on hot coffee and dropped the pot before burying his hand in the snow. "I hate to be the first to tell you," Tucker motioned to the others, "but you don't have a posse now."

"At least Ronnie's handy with a gun," Will said. "I hear tell he beat three men to the draw down around Sante Fe. Carved scallops on his gun each time."

Tucker had heard that rumor, too, and believed it. Ronnie wore his holster low and cut down like a gunny, and his large Spanish rowels screamed *New Mexico* or *Texas.* "The Cauthers won't give him a chance to clear leather."

"Well, then, there's Pasqual. No one crosses him at poker," Will blurted out.

Tucker laughed. "Sure—two feet across the table from him. I admit he's pure snake, killing more than a few who accused him of cheating. But that does us no good across a long field when we're taking fire. And how long's it going to be before he tips too much of his . . . medicine and goes off on one of the others."

Will watched Pasqual cap the bottle on Lydia E. Pinkham's Vegetable Compound—all of twenty percent alcohol—and set it close to where he could grab it whenever the pain hit him again.

"Pasqual needs that for his cough. Got consumption—"

"He needs that 'cause you won't let any of them bring along a bottle of whisky."

Will threw up his hands. "I've still got you."

Tucker stuck his hands in his pockets to warm them and looked across the prairie to the butte. He had seen no movement, nothing to indicate anyone lay in wait. But if Tucker were setting up an ambush, he could ask for no better place that the tall ground overlooking a flat prairie. "I told you, I hired on as a tracker. Not a hired gun."

"That's right; you made a promise to Lorna Moore."

"Where'd you hear that from? Maynard Miles?"

Will took out his hair brush and set his hat aside while he began stroking his head. "Let's just say her father's partner runs off at the mouth when he's got a snoot full."

Tucker stepped closer to Will. Though Will was a couple of inches taller and thirty pounds heavier than Tucker, he stepped back and nearly tripped over a cactus. "Just keep your mouth shut about my relationship with Lorna Moore. It doesn't make any difference if your brother-in-law is the territorial marshal—I'll make sure you never flap your gums again. I'll leave you out here on your own for coyote bait."

"And let the Cauthers keep Jack Worman's whore?"

"That's the *only* thing keeping me riding with your rag-tag bunch. Just make sure you tell these men what we're up against before we go too far."

CHAPTER 4

While the rest of the posse sipped their second cup of coffee and warmed their butts around the fire, Tucker started west, working out Justice Cauther's trail. Which was no easy feat. As Tucker dismounted his Belgian mule, he thought back to what he knew about the man he hunted. When he'd been a cross-border raider during the war, Justice was as fleeting as a fart in a wind storm. He had ridden with Bloody Bill Anderson and William Quantrill, but Justice—it was said—proved even too brutal and uncontrollable for them. Many Union patrols had been sent after him, but he had eluded every one.

Except when he passed out in a Kansas saloon one night after a raid. Tucker snickered, remembering the many times he had tracked wanted Confederate men who had got drunk or distracted in a brothel where the Union troops found them. Troops had captured Justice then, and sent him to the Union's Elmira POW Camp in New York. Four months later he tunneled out of the prison with ten other men, killing two Union officers the night of his escape.

The Pinkertons were tasked with finding him and pasted his likeness over every newspaper and Wanted poster they could hang. They finally located him working as a first mate on a China trader, only to find him gone the day the ship made port back in Boston at the end of the war. Yet even though Confederate guerillas had been pardoned, William Quantrill and Bloody Bill Anderson and Justice Cauther and the likes had never been granted such, and Cauther remained on the run. And just as elusive as ever.

The years after that had the Pinkertons always a step behind Justice, the man's instinct for survival whispered around campfires at night. A bank robbery in St. Louis. The abduction of a prominent Chicago banker; ransom paid. A train derailed in Kansas, the mail car sacked. In each case, Justice had made little effort to hide his face. He wasn't worried. No one had captured him or his gang yet.

He'd moved his operations to the western frontier, and every time Justice hit a stage or robbed passengers on a train, he and his gang were never again seen in the area. The only trail he left was a trail of bodies.

Tucker squatted beside a broken sage branch and smelled it: it had been snapped recently, and he looked west. He had nearly missed the broken branch, and he admired Justice for his ability to hide his trail. An admiration every other posse trying to catch him would never share, Tucker was sure. If he hadn't spotted the occasionally overturned rock, the twig bent into the wind rather than away, the faint scuff beneath the brushed snow, he would not have led the posse this far. They would have been like every other posse trying to find Cauther: riding around in circles with nary a glimpse of the bandits.

Tucker lead his mule, Barney, as he walked, bent over, studying the ground when the mule's ears pricked up. He'd learned long ago that a horse or mule was every bit as good as a dog in alerting a person to danger. Tucker followed the mule's stare to a short rise leading to a shallow valley. Tucker looped Barney's reins around a thick sagebrush and took his rifle from the scabbard. When he made it to the top of the hill, he low-crawled to the edge.

Soft sounds of ghosts passing by, faint scrapes across the frozen ground. A hundred yards away a war party of six Lakota led eight Arikara women tethered together by a rope. Their hands bound by rawhide, they stumbled along to keep up, their bloody bare feet leaving crimson trails in the snow. They winced with each step, yet never cried out to their enemy. One Lakota—a small, wiry warrior—rode as a rear guard. Fresh scalps dangled from his saddle, the dark blood frozen to the white of his pony's withers.

A flanker rode forty yards out, looking for trouble.

And they rode straight toward where the posse rested a quarter mile back.

Tucker scrambled back down the hill and hurriedly untied Barney. He rode the mule the quarter mile back to where the campfire blazed hotter and higher than it should have. Tucker leapt from the saddle and kicked snow over the embers.

"What the hell you do that for?" Ronnie asked. "I was just about to get another cup—"

Tucker took a long step towards Ronnie and clamped a hand over his mouth. The cowhand tried shaking off Tucker's hand, but to little effect. "There's a Sioux war party approaching just over that hill." He chin-pointed in the direction he had come from. When he saw Ronnie's eyes widen, Tucker let go of him. "They're going to be riding not fifty yards past us. Just on the other side where that washout lies. They've got captives, and they're especially wary."

Will grabbed his rifle from the scabbard, while Ronnie and Frank drew their Colts.

Tucker lowered his voice. "Leave the guns holstered. If you want to come out of this with your hair, the best thing we can do is keep the horses quiet and let those Lakota pass."

Will jacked a round into his Winchester. "Including you, there are six of us. And I'd wager we're better armed than they are. Maybe it's time to help the army out—"

"Don't be a fool, Marshal."

Tucker looked hastily around for some place the Indians would not spot them if the flanker rode this way. A hundred yards along a gully, a natural stone archway led to a dry creek bed. If they could get their horses down there, the Indians might pass without spotting them.

Tucker motioned for the others to follow him, and they rode fast and silently through the archway. Tucker pulled up and jumped off the mule.

Will tied his Appaloosa to some rocks. "I still think we can match them—"

"Last thing your . . . posse needs right now is getting into a fight with Lakota."

Ronnie tapped his gun butt. "We can beat them—"

"They'd run circles around you and all the rest." Tucker began to hobble Barney and motioned for the others to do the same. "Those Sioux have lived their whole life as warriors," he told Will. "Can you say the same?"

"Tucker's right," John said. He finished tying rawhide to his mare's legs. "Even the old Indians who come into my blacksmith shop now and again have a hard look about them. If Tucker says the best thing we can do is let them pass, I'm all for it."

"A little scared, old man?" Ronnie said.

"Knock it off," Tucker said, knowing sound carried best on cold days like this. "Another word, and I'll shut your mouth permanently. I got no desire for my scalp to hang with the others on that warrior's saddle."

Tucker walked up the hill separating the posse from the war party and glanced back. He couldn't see the horses or men, and if the posse remained there, they might just get out of this in one piece.

He crept up the hill covered with tall skunkbrush, the orange and brown leaves blending in with his drab denims. In the spring, Indians and settlers would pick the red berries, though bitter, and eat them. Sometimes they steeped them into a tea that Tucker found even more bitter than the raw berries. There were no berries left in this bitter cold, and Tucker carefully crawled through the brush to the top of the hill. He took off his hat and peeked over the edge. The Lakota rode parallel within thirty yards of the hillside. An Arikara woman stumbled on a rock and fell. The Sioux stopped just long enough for the warrior holding the rope to jerk her erect before continuing.

Will scrambled up the hill and lost his footing. Tucker held out his hand and broke his fall. Skunkbrush rattled, and Tucker was certain the Indians had heard Will as he landed on top of his rifle. He brushed dirt off his shirt and breathed hard as he dropped beside Tucker and looked over the hill. "What if they smell our campfire?" he whispered.

"Wind's wrong," Tucker said under his breath. "If we keep our heads down and be quiet, they'll ride by and never even know we're here."

Ronnie crawled on all fours, picking his way through the thick brush, and lay down beside Will. "I've never seen a Sioux except those hanging around town," Ronnie whispered as he looked at the rear guard with the scalps slapping his horse. "What I wouldn't give to have one of those scalps hanging from my saddle," Ronnie said as he cocked his pistol.

"Don't even think about it." Tucker motioned to Ronnie's Colt. "Put that thing away before you get us all killed. Get back to the horses and keep them still."

"Pasqual and John are helping Frank quiet them."

"I think you'd better do what Tucker says," Will said. "From here they actually look pretty fearsome. Maybe Tucker's right—the last thing we need is to get into a gun battle with Sioux." He spat tobacco, and the wind carried it away from him. "We need to find those murderers, not fight with Indians."

The Lakota rode past, silent except for the occasional captive losing her footing, or a horse snorting in protest, or a chuckle as a warrior looked back at the bloody captives. The rear guard looked all about, his head on a swivel, expecting someone to take the women, expecting an ambush. His hand rested on the bow cradled across his lap, and a quiver full of arrows was slung across his shoulders.

He stopped abruptly, his head high, testing the wind.

Tucker flattened himself, and Will and Ronnie followed suit. The warrior pointed his nose to the wind like a coyote that had smelled the faint odor of prey. He turned his horse toward the hill. Tucker motioned for the others to scoot farther down the hillside. "He smells us," Ronnie whispered.

Tucker shook his head. "The wind shifted. He probably smelled the smoke, but he doesn't spot us yet."

"He's coming this way," Will said.

Ronnie drew his gun, and Tucker shook his head. "Don't."

The Lakota stood in the horsehair stirrups, glancing about. He grabbed his bow and notched an arrow while he looked over the prairie. He coaxed his pony a few steps toward the hill of skunkbrush, the man once again testing the wind.

"Toka he?" the lead Indian asked the rear guard as the war party halted. *What's wrong?*

"Sota," the rear guard said.

"He smells our campfire." Tucker lowered his voice just as the Indian trotted his pony toward them. Tucker hugged the ground and watched the Indian ride closer, still unsure if he smelled the smoke from their campfire, unsure just where it came from when . . .

The shot—when it erupted beside him—caused Tucker to jump. Ronnie's first bullet took the Indian mid-chest, and his second round knocked the warrior off his saddle. Will stood and began firing wildly at the other Indians while the rear guard lay painting the frozen snow with his blood.

The rest of the war party kicked their mounts amid loud trilling. Their captives fell, dragged along the ground behind the ponies, and disappeared over a rise fifty yards from where Tucker seethed. He turned to Ronnie and backhanded him. The cowhand dropped his Colt when he fell to the ground, his lip split, his own blood staining his calico shirt. He dove for it and stopped when Tucker jammed his own pistol into Ronnie's temple. "You touch that, and you're a dead man," Tucker said.

Ronnie looked at Tucker, then at the gun, deciding if he should try it.

"Don't be a fool," Will said. He picked up Ronnie's pistol and tucked it in his belt.

"What the hell you doing?" Ronnie said as he gathered his legs beneath him. "That Indian was coming our way. He would have spotted us—"

"He would have ridden on." Tucker looked in the direction the war party had disappeared. "Now they know just where we are."

"It'll be a warning to the others," Will said. "I think I hit one as they were running away."

Ronnie drew his knife and scrambled over the hill toward the dead warrior.

"That damned fool just made our life miserable," said Tucker.

Ronnie bent to the Indian and began sawing his scalp off.

Tucker shook his head. "They'll want revenge for killing one of theirs."

Will thumbed fresh rounds into his Winchester. "Nonsense. You saw the way they high-tailed it over that hill."

Tucker watched Ronnie approaching, a broad smile on his face. He shook blood off the scalp, and it peppered the snow red. "They'll come for us," Tucker said.

Will and Tucker walked down the hill toward where their horses were kept, and Tucker cared little if Ronnie followed.

"What do you think we ought to do?" Will asked.

Tucker looked around at the wash-out they had hidden the horses in, at the stone formation that would provide a good spot to fight from if the war party attacked right now. "We'll hunker down where we're at for the night. Post a guard until morning, for when they come for us."

"You think they will?" Ronnie asked.

"They'll come, damn fool kid," Frank said, pointing at Ronnie approaching with his trophy in his hand. He stood painfully and tucked his pillow under his arm. "They got a beef to settle with us now, and if they figure they can kill us all, they'll have a fine string of horses to show for their dead warrior."

"Shit," Will said, looking around frantically, as if the Lakota were riding over the hill after them this moment. "Tell us what we gotta do."

Tucker took the hobbles of the mule and tightened the britchin strap encircling the mule's rump. He laid his canteen aside and began stripping the saddle of anything that would make noise. "Like I said—keep a guard posted."

"You're not riding out on us?" Ronnie asked.

Tucker swung onto the saddle. "I have half a notion to." He nodded to the scalp hanging from Ronnie's belt. "Enjoy that little souvenir. It might be the last one you ever get." He handed John his Sharps. "Take care of her. Where I'm going, she'll just get in the way."

"Where's that?" Pasqual asked.

Tucker nodded to the hill, in the direction the Indians fled. "If I don't hunt them down first, they'll pick us off one by one at night when we're sleeping. I'm going to count coup first."

Tucker turned his gaze to the setting sun and turned his collar up against the wind. He had seen just where the Indians had fled with their captives. If knew his Lakota, they would hole up where one—perhaps two—men could watch over the women while the other warriors attacked the posse.

Tucker was counting on it. He could put the sneak on two Sioux distracted by their prisoners; more than that, and he might not make it back to the camp.

He walked Barney through the rock formation, when he pulled up short. The wind had shifted again, and for the briefest moment he thought he heard a woman's wailing. The captives? Perhaps, he thought, but Arikara women were tough. They wouldn't give the Lakota the satisfaction of crying out.

Tucker cocked an ear, straining to hear the moan. But the sound was lost to the stiff wind that had shifted once again. Somewhere to the west. Where the Cauthers had ridden.

CHAPTER 5

A rifle shot—from a Winchester, Justice was certain—rose on the wind somewhere to the east from the direction of Ft. Pierre. Justice stood in the stirrups and shielded his eyes with his hands. "Shut that woman up," he snapped at Henny.

Henny slapped Velma. She fell to the ground, holding her face as she spat blood from her mouth. She still had some spunk, Justice noted, as she kicked Henny in the shin. He howled and slapped her again before wrapping his hand around her blood-matted hair. He dragged her to a dead cottonwood and tied her hands with rope. When she tried biting him, he stuffed the same snotty bandana into her mouth.

"Where'd that shot come from?" Justice asked.

"There." Elias pointed across the flat prairie.

"More like there," Gall said, pointing in the direction far from where Gall thought the gunshot originated. Justice knew that a single shot with no reference was hard to figure. But there had been several rifle shots, even a couple of pistol shots, and he'd have thought it easier to range. He cursed the wide-open Dakota Territory that had confounded him once again.

"You go where you figure it came from," Justice told Gall, "and you where you think it was, Elias. But don't roam too far. If y'all haven't seen where those shots came from in a mile or so, beat it back. I don't want any more delays getting the hell out of here."

"What do you want me to do?" Henny asked, his hand under

Velma's dress.

"Keep the whore quiet."

Henny smiled and bent to Velma.

Elias rode into camp, a skiff of snow swirling around his balding head, his horse favoring one front leg. He climbed down and tied his horse to the same cottonwood Henny had tied Velma to earlier. When he heard Elias ride in, Henny topped the slight rise, dragging Velma along the ground behind him. Her dress had bunched up around her waist, but she was too exhausted to pull it down. She shuffled behind Henny as he made his way to the camp fire.

Gall warmed his hands over the flames. He had returned nearly an hour ago without finding where the rifle shot came from. "You have any more luck then I did?"

Elias took out his pocket knife and backed into the horse. He picked the leg up and dug a rock out of the hoof. "You are not going to like this."

"That your horse picked up a stone?" Justice asked.

Elias flicked the stone away and dropped his horse's leg. "That is the least of our worries." He stood and ran his hand along the horse's flank. "Tucker Ashley is riding with some rag-tag posse a couple miles back."

"What?! I thought you said he was whipped into being a storekeeper."

"That new deputy marshal must haf sweet-talked Ashley into tracking for him."

"What do we do now?" Henny said. "I heard that Ashley feller's pure poison—"

"Shut up!" Justice said. "I got to think this out."

He dribbled molasses into his tea and sipped, letting the hot liquid trickle down his throat. It was the only luxury he had to show for so many robberies and so many killings that had brought so few rewards. This take from the saloon keeper in Ft. Pierre was nearly enough to set him and his bunch up for life. If only he could hang on to it.

They should ride on, Justice knew, and to hell with the posse. Reach the Wyoming border, and from there wherever they had a desire to go. But he knew that he needed Tucker Ashley stopped, for that was a man who would follow them when other posses had given up. "Here's what we got to do." Justice nodded to Elias and Gall. "We're going to injun up on those peckerwoods. Give them a good reason not to follow us anymore."

"You mean kill us a lawman or two?"

"As long as it's Ashley."

Gall smiled, and Elias patted Justice on the back. "I was wondering when you were going to want some fun," Elias said. He was untying the reins of his bay when Justice stopped him. "But we're not going to do it just yet. Let them get a good night's rest. Wake up scratching their *cojones* while they wait for their coffee to warm. Then we'll make them wish they'd never signed up."

"What do you want *me* to do?" Henny asked.

"Make sure that woman stays quiet. I don't want to hear even a whimper from her."

Henny grinned and unbuckled his gun belt. "I'll start now."

CHAPTER 6

Tucker reined the mule up short and once again stepped down to look at the drag marks in the snow. When the Indians ran hell-bent-for-election after Ronnie killed one, they had run with a single purpose in mind: revenge for killing one of theirs. Tucker knew this, having lived around them and scouted for the army during a number of campaigns. Though it appeared as if they were running for their lives, in actuality they ran to get clear of the attack. And plan a counter attack. Normally, they would have covered their trail, even in retreat. Unshod ponies—like Tucker's unshod mule—left fainter tracks. Indians would usually be harder to follow.

But this group had women captives to wrestle with.

And the drag marks showed Tucker just where they fled to, even on such a pitch-black night.

He led Barney as he stopped now and again, checking the drag marks, spotting a blood smear against a rock, a piece of long hair where a woman's had caught on a sagebrush or cactus as she was being dragged along.

He bent to the snow and felt the ridges. A spot of blood. Wet. He ran his finger over the blood trail and brought it to his nose. Fresh. Or at least within the past hour. Before long, he would find the Indians, and he tied the mule to a scrub juniper barely surviving at the rim of a coulee. He patted Barney on the neck. "Got to go this one alone," he whispered in his mule's ear.

★ ★ ★ ★ ★

A fire flickered bright on a flat piece of ground overlooked by hills on three sides. Tucker squatted on his haunches and watched, listened. The deathly cold, still night air revealed nothing, and he looked at the hills surrounding the campfire. The women lay close to the fire, rawhide gags in their mouths, lashed together so none could move. The Indians had thought out their plan well—leave the women suffering beside a fire bright enough to draw the white man in. As the *wasicu* swooped in to rescue them, the Lakota would spring the trap. A good plan, Tucker thought. But they hadn't factored him into it.

Squatting fifty yards from the fire, he began systematically searching the hills overlooking the captives. He saw nothing except grass blown by the wind. A thistle blew down the hill and continued across the prairie. Nothing to indicate where the Indians waited above. But they *did* wait for the white men to come.

Tucker staked his life that they were hidden there, waiting.

He moved laterally another ten yards and squatted again when he saw a corner of something move as if possessed—the corner of a blanket wrapped around a man's shoulders. Tucker watched in admiration at the man's discipline. Tucker knew any of Will's posse would have been stomping the ground to generate some circulation, or standing from their assigned spot to keep from freezing, or saying *to hell with it* and walking down to the fire to sit there warming themselves. But these weren't the posse. These were Lakota. These were warriors in the purest sense of the word, men unfazed by the rigors of war. Including the intense cold. And if it hadn't been for a corner of his blanket catching the wind, Tucker might never have spotted him.

He almost regretted what he had to do.

Almost.

He took off his heavy coat and weighted it down with rocks

so the Indian would see it moving, as Tucker had seen the Indian's blanket. He moved laterally once again, planning his route to get to the man. Tucker waited long enough to know this one man had been left behind to ambush any white men following. Tucker had the sinking feeling he often got when fate threw a rock at him he could not duck—with just this one man left behind, the other Lakota had ridden out. For the posse; Tucker was certain.

He took his knife out of the sheath on his belt and held it beside his leg as he began to pick his way up the backside of the hill. Bluestem on the hillsides here mixed with tall grass rustling with the wind, masking his approach. When he got to the top, he paused and took deep, calming breaths. If his estimation was right, the sentry left behind to ambush any rescuers would be sitting in front of a scrub oak not ten yards to Tucker's left.

He set his hat on the ground and felt the ground, picking his way, careful to plant his feet solidly, moving dried branches out of the way before he put his weight down.

He barely made out the tree a couple yards farther. His eyes—adjusted to the night—picked up movement: the blanket once again.

Tucker let his breath out silently, his knife poised for a single slash overhead, and leapt the last few feet to one side of the tree.

Too late he realized the Indian was gone. But his blanket was still there, and Tucker dove for the ground a whisper before a blade *swooshed* in the cold air. Tucker rolled, but the Indian threw himself on him. Big and muscular and used to combat, the Lakota clutched Tucker's throat, squeezing, the air choked from him as the Indian brought the blade down.

Tucker drove his knee into the Indian's groin. The man grunted once, but fought through the pain as he dove for Tucker again.

He lashed out with a wicked jab that landed on the Indian's face. Blood sprayed from his nose, and when he hesitated a moment too long, Tucker plunged his knife into the man's chest. He ripped his blade up violently and rolled away.

In death, the Indian slashed the air, back and forth in front of him, Tucker's knife sticking out of his chest until his movement slowed, then stopped altogether, and he collapsed to the ground.

Tucker put a boot against the dead man's chest and pulled his knife free. He wiped it on the blanket, retrieved his hat, and stumbled down the hill to where he left his coat. By the time he found it, the chill had reached deep into his bones. He could only imagine what the captives were feeling right now. In a moment he would ask them, right after he cut them loose.

Chapter 7

Tucker rode the hill overlooking the camp just as the sun peeked above the tall grass. He reined his mule up short and studied the camp. A quarter mile along the coulee, in the safety of the rock formation that provided cover, bodies lay around a dying campfire. Men stirred under tarps and blankets, and Tucker took out his binoculars. He was a cautious man—his captain in the Bucktails thought a little too cautious, even though it had saved his life more than once in the war. He glassed the camp.

And cursed under his breath.

Pasqual sat apart from the others, leaning against the rocks, his chin on his chest. So, he had the cocktail guard—the last one to stand watch. How long he had slept, Tucker had no way of knowing.

But it had been fully long enough that two horses were missing.

He made a loose circle around the camp until he picked up sign of barefoot ponies: Lakota. During the night, they had ridden into camp, stolen two horses as easily as Tucker spotted their tracks just now, and left as quietly as they came. While Tucker was putting the sneak on their camp to wound as many as he could during the night, the Indians stole the horses. At least, Tucker thought, the Indians would have fits when they found their captives had escaped.

Tucker rode Barney down the hill to the camp, and no one stirred even as he dismounted. He walked to Pasqual and kicked him in the leg. Pasqual jumped, startled, and his hands went for his pistols nestled in the shoulder holsters.

"Leave those damned guns alone," Tucker said. "You've done enough damage already."

"What's the commotion?" Will threw his tarp back and crawled out from under his blankets. He put his raccoon coat on as he bent to the fire, laying more wood on the dying embers. "How'd the fire die down so quick?"

Tucker nodded to Pasqual. "Ask your night guard here. He let the fire go like he let the horses go."

"Horses?" Ronnie asked. He poked his head from under his blanket.

"That's right—horses," Frank said. He stomped his feet to seat his boots, and grabbed his butt pillow before moving closer to the fire. "Looks like we're two short." He nodded to where the remaining horses stood hobbled.

"What?" Will said. "How the hell—"

"Lakota," Tucker said. He walked to the horses the Indians had left last night and picked up rawhide hobbles that had been sliced cleanly. He squatted, brushing snow away until he spotted the raiders' sign. Three, perhaps four, Indians had stood apart from the sleeping posse, watching. They had probably waited until Pasqual dozed off, knowing a man has a hard time staying awake in those hours just before dawn.

Tucker walked back to the fire, holding the sliced hobbles in his clenched fist. He tossed them at Pasqual, and they hit him in the chest. "Don't you just beat all. Couldn't stay awake for one night."

Pasqual flung the hobbles on the ground. "If it makes you feel better, one of the horses they stole was mine."

"They took my buckskin, too," Ronnie said. He stepped closer to Pasqual. "How the hell long were you asleep?"

Frank stepped between them. "No sense killing each other—

they're gone now."

"How could they have sneaked in here and stolen them right under our noses?" John asked. He used the rocks to stand, and hitched his trousers up over his belly. "They had to have made noise."

"And why didn't they kill one or all of us while they were at it?" Will asked. "It looks like they were close enough."

Tucker had wondered the same thing, and there was only one explanation. "Those Sioux wanted revenge, all right. But they didn't want to chance that some of you would wake up and start shooting. My guess is they're just one step ahead of an army patrol and didn't want to risk soldiers hearing gunshots. So they led two horses away, knowing it would put a hell of a hardship on us."

Will stared at the horses. "But how—"

"They're Lakota," Tucker said simply.

"Now what are we going to do?" Will asked.

"Double up," Tucker said.

Ronnie spat a string of tobacco juice, and some dribbled onto his prized scalp still hanging from his belt. "I'll be damned if I'll ride with you on that mule."

Tucker smiled. "My thoughts exactly. Me and Barney go solo. You figure out among yourselves how you want to double up."

Tucker fished coffee out of his saddlebags and scooped snow into the coffeepot. He set it on the rocks, and soon steam arose from it. "After I have something to warm my insides, I'll see about finding some game. I think I saw a small herd of antelope as I was riding here."

When the coffee was ready, Tucker filled his cup and walked a ways off from the others. *How the hell did I get mixed up with these fools?* The only one with any trail sense was Frank, and he was too stove-in and sore in the backside to be of much use.

Tucker would have turned on his heels and gone back to Ft. Pierre. It mattered little to him if Wilson Dawes and his posse wandered aimlessly until they got lost and were at the mercy of another Lakota war party.

Except for Velma. The memory of her and Jack walking the streets, giggly-happy like little kids, stuck in his mind. Against his best sense, he'd stay with Will.

Tucker tossed his grounds out and swished snow in the cup to clean it as he watched a herd of fifteen or so antelope graze the tall grass at the foot of a line of hills. Tucker hadn't eaten anything since joining the posse except pemmican and some buffalo jerky he always kept in his bags. And he was certain the others hadn't either. A fat pronghorn would bring them around, perhaps give them enough gumption to continue despite losing the horses.

He turned and started back to get his rifle, when hooves behind him slapped the frozen ground. He turned and watched as the antelope ran across the prairie in front of the hills as if chased by a coyote.

Except there was no coyote in sight.

And Tucker took off at a dead run toward the safety of the rocks.

Chapter 8

The small herd of pronghorn ran by as if chased by a cougar and disappeared over a hill as Justice settled behind a rock outcropping. He peeked around a boulder just far enough to see that Elias had crawled into position. He sat with his back against a clump of switchgrass while he blew warm air onto his gun hand. The wind had picked up in time with a drop in temperature, and Elias had grudgingly wrapped a scarf around his face and ears. He had pulled his duster around him—compliments of a Wells Fargo stage they had robbed over Yankton way this spring—and he flashed the sign at Justice. *Elias was ready.*

Justice had spotted Elias easily, but he strained to see where Gall hid himself somewhere atop the next hill over. But then the Confederate sharpshooter was savvy enough that no one on the rim of the valley or the posse below would spot him. Unless he wished it. Gall had been a sharpshooter his entire war career, and even he never knew how many successful stalks he'd had, how many Union soldiers he had killed that had never seen him or that fancy rifle he used.

Justice carefully moved out from the boulder so he could watch the posse in the shallow valley below. Two men stood guard around a string of horses, smoking and joking without a care in the world. An older man beside them sat on a dead stump, the fringes of his red pillow flapping under the man's scrawny butt. The younger of the two men had his hands jammed inside his waistcoat staring at the fire, a blood-frozen scalp dangling from his belt. A tall man in a raccoon coat ran from around the rock formation and spoke to the posse. They laughed and looked over to where Justice and his men were hidden before going back to warming themselves over the fire.

Gall had been the one to spot the dead Indian a short way from the posse, and Justice put his men on high alert. His interest was Tucker Ashley and the posse he rode with, not a Sioux war party out for blood. The Sioux wouldn't forget one of theirs had been killed and scalped and left to the prairie scavengers—coyotes and badgers and bobcat hungry for any meal they could get in this cold. Even a corpse with no hair. But Justice had something more lively in mind for the lawmen than worrying about a passing band of Lakota.

The rocks below prevented him from seeing the rest of the posse, and he only caught moving men's shadows now and again in the rising sun. Whoever had chosen the site to hole up from the Indians knew how to read terrain. It was a place Justice himself would have chosen to defend from. But this was the time of the day when men groggily woke from sleep, and the first things on their minds was coffee and something to put in their gullet. This was the time of day when intense cold was being shaken off, fires burned hot, and minds thought of anything besides being ambushed.

When Justice planned the trap, he and Elias agreed that Gall would start the party. With that fancy rifle of his, Gall's first shot would take out one of the lawmen. Preferably Tucker Ashley. And then it was Katie bar the door, and pepper as many as they could in the shortest amount of time.

Justice eased back behind the rock again and rested his rifle between the branches of a sagebrush. He breathed slowly, willing his heart to slow. As many times as he had set an ambush for a Union patrol—or a posse—the anticipation of killing his enemy always made his heart beat quick and thick, his trigger finger anxious for that first volley of rounds down-range.

Even though he knew Gall would shoot first, the sound startled Justice for the briefest moment. He recovered and began firing and levering shells into his gun as fast as Elias was doing fifty yards over. Gall was slower to reload, but when he did and fired again, Justice heard the harsh *thud* of his bullet impacting something or someone even from this far away.

The men below dove for cover, unsure at first where the attack came from. Justice spotted a leg out from cover, and he shot at it. The man jerked back, and Justice fired two more follow-up shots at the same place. One man writhed beside the fire just before another dragged him to the safety of the rocks.

Justice and Elias continued firing until no more targets were visible and then backed up to rendezvous over the hill behind them.

They were untying their horses when Gall ambled down from his high spot. "Did you get Ashley?" Justice asked when Gall arrived.

Gall bit off a chunk of tobacco and pocketed the rest of the plug. "I *think* it was Ashley."

"Think?" Justice asked. "You don't know for certain."

Gall carefully slipped his rifle in the saddle scabbard. "I shot at the tallest man there. I'd wager that was Ashley," he smiled. "And I'd wager he'll be no more trouble to us."

Chapter 9

Tucker struggled to drag John to the far side of a large boulder, a wide swath of blood trailing him in the snow. Two more bullets impacted the rock beside where John had gone down a moment ago, pelting Tucker's cheek. He called over his shoulder to Ronnie, "Fetch my saddlebags."

Ronnie ignored him and fired at puffs of smoke that rose from somewhere up the hill to the west.

"Do it now!" Tucker yelled. "John needs some doctorin'."

Ronnie crawled to Tucker's saddlebags, while Tucker bent to John. His contorted face showed the pain he was in, but he said nothing as Tucker sliced the blacksmith's trousers half way up his side to examine the wound. A rifle round had entered John's leg just above the knee and traveled up the leg before exiting his hip. "Anyone else hit?" Tucker yelled above the din of the shooting.

"Son's-a-bitches shot a hole right through my new hat," Will said. He leaned around the rocks, snapped two quick shots up the hill, and ducked back again.

"I got my face peppered good from some rocks chips," Pasqual said. He held his two small gambler's guns in front of him.

"Those things are as useless as teats on a boar hog," Frank said. He dropped beside Pasqual and stuck his rifle barrel between a rock and a downed cottonwood. He fired four quick shots from his .44 Henry before fumbling in his pocket for more ammunition. "As far away as they are, we're lucky to hit them at all."

Ronnie flung Tucker his saddlebags, and they skidded in the snow. Ronnie returned to watching the hillside, his own rifle poised to shoot at anything. If he actually saw a target.

Tucker was cutting John's trousers higher up the hip when the fat man stopped him. "You ain't gonna' tell the others?" he lowered his voice.

Tucker paused. "Tell them what?"

John looked around Tucker before he pulled his shirt up. Under John's trousers a pair of women's underthings peeked out, lovely yellow flowers imprinted on bright red cloth.

"What the hell?"

John shrugged. "They're a lot cooler to wear when I'm working the forge all day." A slight smile spread across his pain-wracked face. "And they make me feel good all under. Kinda' got used to them." He looked past Tucker. "You ain't gonna' tell anyone, are you?"

Tucker suppressed a grin. "Whatever makes you feel . . . manly. I'm not going to mention it," Tucker said as he fished around in his saddlebags for his patch kit.

A stray bullet hit against the rocks in back of where John and Tucker lay and ricocheted off the stone. Will scurried, bent over, and dropped beside them, fumbling in his cartridge belt for fresh Winchester rounds. "Must be a dozen of those red bastards up there."

"More than that," Pasqual hollered. "I thought they didn't have many guns."

"They're not Indians," Tucker said. "Those are white men up that hillside. And there's only three of them."

Pasqual craned his head to look back at Tucker. "You a seer or something? Only a seer can know things he can't see. Ran into a few of them down New Orleans way during the war."

Tucker stuffed his bandana into John's leaking wound to stop the bleeding while he grabbed his needle and thread from his kit. The last time he'd used his kit was to stitch a prolapsed cow he'd found wandering around the river town last calving season. John wasn't a cow—though he might be as big as one. Tucker figured John wouldn't mind any if he used the same kit. "Three distinct guns: a Spencer.44 and a .44-40. And something else I heard a time or two during the war—a Whitworth."

Frank whistled. "That's what I thought." The firing up the hill had stopped, but the old cowboy remained prone behind his rifle and behind the safety of the rocks. "No mistaking that whining as the bullets come at you. We ran into those in Spotsylvania. Damned Confederate sharpshooters kept us pinned down from a half mile away." He laid his rifle on the ground and grabbed his tobacco pouch from inside his waistcoat, oblivious to the bullets hitting the boulders above his head, the occasional rock chip falling down on him. He began rolling a smoke while he watched the hillside. "But whoever's shooting a Whitworth could have equipped himself with something easier to carry—a Sharps. Maybe a Ballard."

"He's probably comfortable with it," Tucker said. Folks said the same thing about him—why carry that clumsy Sharps when a Henry or Winchester would be so much handier. Because Tucker was used to the big fifty and knew just where it hit.

"You fellas don't mind having a weapons discussion when I'm not leaking all over the ground." John's face had paled with the loss of blood, but he retained his humor. He'd need it, Tucker thought, as he handed Pasqual the needle with thread dangling from it. "Crawl over to the fire and stick it in there until it gets red hot. And don't burn the thread."

"Why me all the time?" Pasqual said.

"Because the next person I sew up might be you."

"You got to dig the slug out of me first?" John asked between teeth clenched tight.

"Slug passed through you," Tucker answered. "You were lucky."

"Funny I don't feel lucky," John said, a grimace crossing his face. "But I wish I had some of Harmy's good sipping whisky he kept behind the bar to dull the pain."

"Pasqual," Tucker shouted above the noise. "Grab me that bottle of patent medicine from your bag."

"But it's my last bottle."

"You heard him," Will said. "Even though I'm not a drinking man, I wouldn't want to tough it out with what Tucker's about to do with nothing to help the pain."

Pasqual chanced a look around the rocks before he scrambled for his saddlebags leaning against his bedroll. He grabbed his bottle of Pinkhams Compound and tossed it over.

Tucker uncorked it and handed it to John. He chugged the bottle and wiped his mouth with the back of his hand. "Now I'm ready," John said, and Tucker became aware the firing had stopped.

"Maybe they ran off," Ronnie said. He started to stand when Frank grabbed him by the suspenders and yanked him to the ground. "Hell of a way to see if they're still there—standing up like a damn fool. But if you really want to . . ." Frank let go of Ronnie, but he remained behind the cover of the rocks. "Now keep your head down and take that needle over there."

Pasqual crawled back to Tucker and handed him the horse needle. When it had cooled enough to grab, Tucker took his bandana out of the hole and began stitching John's wound closed. By the time he'd finished, it had been twenty minutes without any more incoming rounds.

Will drew his legs under him and sat with his back against the rocks as he chanced a quick peek around. "I think they're gone," he said. "You figure that was the Cauthers?" he asked Tucker.

Tucker sprinkled water on sage that he'd ground up to make a poultice for John's wound. "Of course it was the Cauthers. When Ronnie there decided he had to have that Indian scalp, the gang must have been close enough to hear the shots."

"He would have discovered us—"

"What are you talking about, the Cauthers?" Frank stood painfully and looked about the camp for his pillow. "No one said anything about the Cauthers."

Will looked down as he reloaded his rifle.

"Marshal," Frank said. "You look at us."

"Yeah—Wilson Dawes," Ronnie said. "You look at us."

Will's eyes darted between Ronnie and Frank.

Pasqual walked bent over and squatted beside the others. "That true, Will?"

"Tell them." Tucker cut off the excess string and wiped blood off the needle on his denims before stuffing it back into his saddle bag. "They got a right to know what we're up against."

"All right," Will said. He stood and paced in front of the others. "Those men who murdered Harmy and kidnapped Velma belong to the Cauther Gang."

Ronnie stepped closer to Will and looked up at him. "Why the hell didn't you level with us?"

"Would you have signed on if you knew who we were after?"

"Not for a dollar a day." Ronnie took a pouch of Bull Durham from his pocket. His hand shook as he trickled tobacco onto a paper. "Not for ten times that much."

"You act like the Cauthers are invincible," Will said. As if to punctuate this, he stepped away from the cover of the rocks. But Tucker was certain the shooters had long fled their hillside ambush site.

"Tucker, what do you think our chances are with the Cauthers?" Frank glared at Will. "I think we have a right to know. Should we go back to Ft. Pierre or continue, 'cause I'm not going to get my ass shot off for a dollar a day."

John groaned, pain from the ordeal covering his face with sweat that would soon freeze. Tucker dabbed at the fat man's cheek with his bandana.

"Yeah," Pasqual said. "Just what are our chances?"

John's head rolled to one side, and Tucker propped it up with his saddle blanket. He rubbed his hands with snow and wiped the rest of John's blood off on his trousers while he thought about the question.

He stood and faced Will and the others. "Here's the facts: the last time a posse caught up with the Cauthers, they slaughtered them. They left one deputy alive to go back to Cheyenne and tell folks what happened. Justice Cauther and his men—the deputy claimed—actually enjoyed killing the posse. Justice himself executed two wounded men as they lay bleeding but alive and pleading."

"So, we got no chance?" Frank asked.

Tucker looked around at the wounded blacksmith; at the two suspected rustlers; at the flamboyant gambler at home at a poker or faro table. But none of these men should have been riding the trail after Justice Cauther and his gang. And the leader of these merry men—a school-teacher-turned-deputy marshal—was only appointed to the position because his brother-in-law wanted him out of his hair. "The chances of all of us living through this"—Tucker nodded to John, who thrashed into a fitful sleep—"are slim."

"Tucker!" Will said.

Tucker shrugged and bent to the fire. He laid more kindling on the glowing coals. "They deserve to know their odds."

"Well that's just great," Pasqual said and turned to Ronnie. "If you hadn't shot that Indian, the Cauthers wouldn't have even known we were on their trail."

"If you hadn't fallen asleep, we'd still have enough horses."

"You son of a bitch."

Ronnie backed away, and his hand dropped beside his holster. "You want to push it, fancy man?"

Pasqual shucked his jacket, and his hands hovered by his twin shoulder holsters. "Any time, cow thief—"

"Enough!" Tucker stepped toward Ronnie. "Cool your heels. Pasqual is right, though—they wouldn't have known we were this close if you hadn't wanted that souvenir." Tucker snatched the scalp and tossed it aside.

"You taking sides?" Ronnie spat tobacco juice and backed away. His hand twitched above his gun butt.

"If you skin that Colt, you'll be the second man I killed today," Tucker said.

Ronnie smiled and turned as if to walk away when his hand dropped to his gun. By the time he'd drawn and spun toward Tucker, Tucker's gun was already out and pointed at Ronnie's chest. "You're a damned fool, kid. Now, you want to be planted here or live to see the sun set today?"

Frank stepped between them. "He don't mean nothing, Tucker," he said as he slapped Ronnie's hand from his gun butt. "Do you?"

Ronnie had turned as white as the surrounding snow as he starred wide-eyed at Tucker's Remington .44 centered on his chest. "Some other time," he stammered, too proud to admit that he'd come a heartbeat away from death.

Frank dragged Ronnie aside, and Tucker slowly decocked his gun and holstered it. "Me and Ronnie will light out in the morning," Frank said over his shoulder.

"I'll be with you," Pasqual said. "Marshal Dawes can't pay me enough to go after the Cauthers."

"Now wait a minute," Will said, backing up to the fire. "The

Cauthers are long gone by now. They won't figure we'll continue after them after that"—he nodded to John. "I still need a posse."

"Don't relax too soon," Tucker said. He stepped from the rocks and looked about. The Cauthers had planned their ambush well: setting up on the high ground, with interlocking fields of fire. The only thing that had saved the posse was their position among the rocks. "They could still be waiting for us over the next hill."

"We'll be ready next time," Will said.

"That's what you said about the Lakota, and look what they did."

"But they're long gone, too."

Tucker shook his head. He wasn't born to suffer fools, but here he was. "Don't be so sure."

CHAPTER 10

Tucker returned from looking over the prairie. He worked out a route that would take him to where the Cauthers had staged their ambush. He was almost certain the gang fled right after the echoing shots died down, but he couldn't be certain. Tucker was—after all—a cautious man.

When he rode back into camp, he expected to see bedrolls and tarps secured behind saddles, and men filled with fresh coffee ready to head in the direction Tucker told them. Instead, it was all Will could do to stop the men from bolting.

"Tell them," Will blurted out when he saw Tucker. "Tell them we can't spare any horses."

Ronnie tied his bedroll with a leather pigging string. "I'm outta' here—"

"On what?" Tucker asked.

Ronnie nodded to the horses. "I'll borrow one of those. Leave it back in town—"

"We can't spare even one horse," Will said. "I tried telling them that."

"How about John's mare? He's about gone anyway. He won't be needing it—"

"He's about to crawl over there and put a boot in your butt," John said. He propped himself up with his arm. "You take my Sadie, and I'll snap your neck like a twig."

"Like hell you well, old man," Ronnie said.

"I'm coming with you," Pasqual said.

They stopped short when they heard Tucker's pistol cocking. "We're short horses; there's no getting around that. We can't spare any, but if you want to walk back, I can't stop you."

Pasqual and Ronnie faced Tucker. "You know we wouldn't have a chance on foot if those Sioux got onto out trail."

Tucker shrugged. "If you try to take any of the horses, this gun of mine will make certain that no one has to double up. Now what's it going to be—trying to take a horse, or leaving your blood where you stand?"

Ronnie glared at Tucker. "One day soon, you and me will do the dance—"

"We already did that, remember?" Tucker said. "But you didn't know the tune."

"You think you can ride?" Will asked John.

"I can sit my horse, all right."

Tucker stepped behind John and wrapped his arms around him. He grunted with the effort, but John stood on his one good leg. "Looks like I'm going to have to mount Indian," he said, and Tucker agreed. With John's left leg so severely wounded, he couldn't put weight on it; wouldn't be able to use the stirrup to climb on Sadie. He would have to mount his mare from the right side, like Indians mounted their ponies.

But Sadie wasn't used to John sitting the saddle from the opposite side. She humped, and her teeth nipped at John's coat before Tucker draped his coat over her eyes. Tucker eased John onto the horse, and he gingerly settled into his seat before motioning to Pasqual. He stood on the stump and swung his leg over the saddle behind John.

"What a bunch of horse shit," Pasqual said. "Riding behind someone like I was a squaw or something."

John winced in pain when Pasqual grabbed his belt to hold on. "Don't put pressure on that side."

"See?" Ronnie said. "John can't ride. Let me take his horse back to town—"

"Just shut that pneumonia hole and get up here." Frank positioned his pillow so it centered the saddle before he eased himself down. He held out his hand and swung Ronnie behind him onto the horse. Range men don't like riding double, but Ronnie had no choice.

Cowboys weren't Indians.

Tucker had lived with the Crow the year he came west after the war. When they found themselves short of horses for every man—like when the Lakota ventured into Crow country on a horse-stealing raid—they simply teamed up: one warrior rode while the other ran beside the pony, grasping the mane, the tail, anything that would keep him erect and running. And when he could not go any farther, they switched. But Tucker couldn't see these men doing anything like that. A few of them could barely sit a horse.

John clutched the saddle horn like he was milking an old cow. He fidgeted as he tried to relieve pressure off his injured leg and hip.

"You sure you can ride?" Tucker asked.

John jerked his thumb behind him. "With those two vultures anxious to take my Sadie, I can. Just might need a little help now and again."

"That's enough," Will said. He had brushed his hair and carefully donned his Montana Peak. *He's sure a pretty man,* Tucker thought. *Next thing he'll be running for office.* "Quit you're bitchin'," Will told Pasqual. "It's your own damned fault for falling asleep." He pulled his collar up against the biting wind. "If you'd been awake, you'd be riding your own horse now. Like Tucker said, you're lucky they didn't slit your throat."

"If Pasqual had been awake," Tucker said as he rode his mule past the others, "they would have just killed him to keep him quiet." He snickered at Pasqual jostling behind John. "Just the luck of a gambler I suppose."

"Well, as soon as we get someplace we can buy horses," Ronnie said, "we're done with your posse."

"Fair enough," Will said. "But for now, you ride for the brand, so to speak—at a dollar a day." He stopped his Appaloosa beside Tucker and lowered his voice. "With two horses down, what's our chances?"

"Of finding the Cauthers? Little. It takes a good horse to survive where we're going, and that's with only one rider. We'll be slowed down so much that the only way we'll find Justice is if he stops and waits for us."

"And just making it back?"

Tucker took a sip from his water bladder and slipped it back over his saddle horn. "Horses need enough grain or hay to keep fit. If Justice continues the direction he's going, grass will be at a premium." He motioned to Will's fine horse. "You bring a feed bag for him?"

Will guffawed. " 'Course not."

"Well, that's what he's used to."

"Appaloosas can go wherever a man wants—"

"When was the last time you took this animal on anything but a pleasure ride with some lady beside you?"

Will looked away.

"That's what I thought," Tucker said. "It might be a blessing that two of your men are doubled-up—means their horses will be slowed. Might give your Appaloosa more time to graze."

"Well, you're no better off with that." Will pointed to the mule. "Skinny legs, and tiny hooves; he'll be lucky if he can keep up with us."

"You taught school before your brother-in-law appointed you deputy marshal?"

Will's chest puffed slightly. "In Sioux City."

"So, you had little opportunity to . . . live the west."

"What *are* you getting at?"

"That you have little experience with horses. Or mules." Tucker patted Barney's neck. "Only critter who can stay on the trail eating anything from fence posts to cactus to loco weed is a mule. When your horse refuses water from an alkali spring, Barney here will drink it and live with the consequences. And when those bright new shoes on that Appaloosa slip over rocks, my mule will keep upright and keep going." He turned Barney toward the hills where their attackers had lain in ambush this morning. "Stay put," he told the others. "I don't want you mucking up any tracks the Cauthers left."

While the rest of the posse remained at the base of the hill, Tucker rode to the top. He had dismounted between two small mounds when he spotted a depression where someone had lain, the man's body heat melting the snow.

Tucker looked down at their camp site. The shooter up here had as good a position to fire from as he could have had, and Tucker was just grateful more men weren't hit besides John.

He squatted beside the depression and brushed the fresh snow away. A piece of paper no bigger than his thumbnail lay buried beneath, and Tucker picked it up—a burnt scrap of paper. He massaged it between his thumb and finger and felt the linen imbedded, then he brought it to his nose. Gunpowder. The shooter shot paper-patched bullets in his Whitworth. It was paper partially burnt after it left the muzzle that Tucker found. The shooter had been schooled to wring the most accuracy out of his rifle. Tucker filed the information in the back of his mind—when they caught up with the Cauthers, this man might be even more dangerous than Justice.

He dropped the paper and walked a semicircle around where the shooter had lain. Tucker looked into the sun and spotted a rock overturned—with packed dirt underneath where the man had kicked it over when he left. Tucker lightly brushed the snow with his hand until he spotted a boot scuff in the hard earth, then another. He stood and arched his back, stretching. He had the man's stride, and he had the direction he had fled after the ambush.

The Cauthers continued to flee west.

He mounted the mule, trying to place himself in the Cauthers' position. They could have ridden away this morning. Hide their back trail, as Justice did so well, and the posse would never have been able to catch up with them. Only Tucker had been able to work out their tracks to lead the posse after the gang. Was it because they had become so hateful that they were willing to murder anyone, any time, for pure pleasure? Tucker thought it more than that. Killers robbed to get money; to live a particular life that pleased them. When the money ran out, they robbed again. The Cauthers could have been halfway out of the territory if they hadn't taken the time to ambush the posse this morning. Only Tucker's selection of a campsite had saved them. But it might not do so the next time.

He had turned Barney to head down the hillside where the posse waited when something caught his eye in a valley to the south. The valley where he had killed the brave. Where he'd freed the Arikara captives.

He grabbed his binoculars and glassed the high grass. Four Lakota rode toward where the posse had camped last night. War paint covered their faces and necks and the withers of their ponies. They rode fast, unencumbered by the women. Either they had found the Arikara captives, or the women had gotten away; Tucker wasn't sure. What he was certain of, though, was that once the Indians arrived at the posse's campsite, they would quickly work out their tracks. And they would come after the posse with a vengeance.

CHAPTER 11

When the sun started to peek through the thick snow clouds overhead, the posse arrived at what was left of the Cauthers' camp. They had taken no effort to hide where they had slept for the night, as if they had no concern the posse would follow.

Will climbed down from his Appaloosa and stood beside Tucker. "Pretty sloppy." He grabbed his kit and rolled a smoke, lighting it on campfire embers that still glowed amber. "You'd think they would hide their camp better. Guess the Cauthers are vulnerable after all."

"They never figured we'd keep following them after that dusting they gave us yesterday . . ." Tucker lifted his head, testing the air. A dangerously familiar odor drifted past his nose, then was lost to the wind.

"Or maybe they were just worried enough they lit out, figuring we'd catch up with them and offer a little dusting of our own," Will said loud enough for the others to hear. As if he were pumping up his pathetic posse.

The odor came again, teasing Tucker for the briefest time. An odor he couldn't quite put the tip of his nose on.

Ronnie climbed down and stretched, and Pasqual swung down from behind John.

"Give John a hand," Tucker said. "He needs to stretch that leg out some."

"Now I got to help the fat man—"

"That's enough," Will said. "Earn your dollar and give John a hand."

Tucker's mule picked its head to the wind and backed away from the short hill on the backside of the Cauthers' camp. Tucker climbed down and followed Barney's wild-eyed stare. Tucker handed the reins to Ronnie and walked to a slight rise, the putrid smell becoming stronger.

Blood.

As many times as he'd been around it, Tucker never got used to the putrid smell of blood. Fallen snow had covered tracks, yet broken sage and overturned rocks showed where someone had been dragged toward the hill. Tucker reached the top and stared down at the dead body.

Velma Hart lay beside some cactus. Blood frozen to her dress tainted the lively print fabric pulled up over her waist, and her ripped underthings lay a few feet from her. A leather thong still circled her neck, and she looked up at the sky, her eyes fixed open, her tongue protruding and swollen.

Tucker took off his hat as he thought of the last time he'd seen Velma. She'd sung a solo at the Bucket of Blood, walking among the rowdies afterwards, flirting before she settled on Jack Worman seated in one corner of the saloon. She'd flirt with no one again.

"Jesus," Will said. He walked up the hill and stood beside Tucker looking down at the corpse. "Why now? Why kill her here?"

Tucker had no answers as he walked the last few steps toward Velma. He squatted beside her and pulled her dress down. "Give me your bandana." He held out his hand.

"What for?" Will asked. "It came all the way from St. Louis. It's real silk—"

"All the more reason. Velma deserves the best. Hand it over."

Will took the bandana from around his neck and handed it to

Tucker, who carefully wrapped it around Velma's eyes. "Tell the others to get up here. Except John. He's in no shape to bury her."

Tucker stood and waited for the others to plod up the hill. Will had posed a question Tucker could not answer. The Cauthers had kept Velma alive these last days until now. Were they worried she'd slow them down and killed her? Or when they raped her, had they gone too far? With Velma dead, the reason Tucker had agreed to track for the posse had disappeared. He could turn back now, return to Lorna and the mercantile. Her father would be debarking from the boat any day, and they could go on with their lives.

But the brutal sight of Velma caused him to pause. In the end, it came down to his growing hatred for Justice Cauther. Tucker would stay with the posse.

The others trudged past Tucker. Pasqual gasped when he saw Velma and turned to the side and puked. Ronnie stepped away from her, but Tucker stopped him. "Get down there and help us bury her."

"I'm not getting close—"

"Just do it." Frank shoved Ronnie ahead of him. "It's the right thing to do."

"You, too, Will," Tucker said as he began gathering rocks. He would have preferred burying her decent-like. But the frozen ground would take too much time to break through. And he intended to find Justice Cauther.

When they finished stacking rocks around the body, they all stood silent, looking at Will to say something. "Your daddy was a deacon in the church, wasn't he?" he asked Tucker. "Maybe you can say a few words."

Tucker held his Stetson as he looked solemnly at the pile of stones covering Velma. His father *had* been a deacon in their

Pennsylvania church and could quote scripture all day as he plowed his field beside his son, or during planting season, or harvesting their corn crop, or when he was gutting a deer to bring home to the larder. But quoting scripture wasn't hereditary. Tucker hadn't set foot in a church since his parents died when their buggy overturned coming back from Sunday services. His captain in the Bucktails had been a devout man, up until a Confederate minié ball pierced his heart. But Tucker wasn't.

Tucker cleared his throat, surprised that he recalled as much Bible teaching as he did. He spoke briefly about how the Lord welcomed even soiled doves like Velma, a good person despite overcharging her drunk customers in her crib above the Bucket now and again. When he finished, Tucker said a few lines from St. John that he remembered his father recite and gave a muted "amen."

The posse moved silently away from the body. Frank was the last to don his hat, and he looked sadly down at the pile of rocks. "I had a daughter once," he said. "She would have been Velma's age if the Comanches hadn't taken her. Good girl she was—"

The whine of a Whitworth bullet cutting the afternoon air reached them a heartbeat after the sickening *thud.* Pieces of coat flew from Frank as the bullet exited his chest, and he was dead and toppled over before his eyes could blink in astonishment.

The rest of the posse dove for the cover of rocks or the few scrub oaks lining the hill. Pasqual peeked over the hill as another bullet tore up the ground where he'd stood a moment before. Their horses—spooked from the sudden incoming noise—fought John below as he held their reins. "Hang tight to them," Tucker called to John over the screams of the posse men.

Tucker's mule, calm even amid chaos, pawed the ground.

Tucker ran to Barney and skinned the Sharps rifle from the scabbard. He crawled to where Will poked his head over the hillside. "Where the hell did that shot come from?" Will's .44-40 was in his hand, as if it could reach out to the shooter.

"Don't waste your ammo," Tucker told him. "He's well out of range of that Winchester."

Tucker estimated the range where he saw the puff of smoke and adjusted his peep sight to five hundred yards. He fired off a .50 round and quickly opened the action. The long shell casing dropped onto the ground. Hissing steam rose off it as it melted snow where it lay. "Across that valley," Tucker said. "Same SOB who started the party yesterday." Tucker set the back trigger, then touched the tip of his finger on the front one. The Sharps bucked again and moved Tucker back several inches in the snow.

He snapped the loading gate lever downward and shucked another round out. He fired two more quick rounds—as quick as a buffalo gun can fire—at where he was sure the shooter hid.

The horses broke from John's grasp and ran off across the prairie.

Ronnie crawled toward Will and dropped beside him. He looked up at the hillside. "Think the shooter's still there?"

"Can't say," Will answered. "Maybe he's gone. Been a few minutes since he shot."

"Well, I hope so, 'cause I'd like to get my sights on that bastard for killing Frank."

"You pop your head up too far," Tucker said as he thumbed fresh cases out of his cartridge belt, "and you might just join Frank."

"Why ain't the others shooting?" Pasqual asked. He hadn't even pulled his own short-barreled guns. "Last time it sounded like an army was attacking us."

"Because they're not there," Tucker said. He opened the loading lever and blew into the action of the Sharps to expel smoke while he continued scanning the land across the valley. "This one was left to harass us. Kill as many as he could. He'll join the others down the trail, no doubt."

After twenty minutes with no more incoming fire, Tucker figured the shooter had fled. He stood and headed down the hill to his mule. "We got us another body to bury," he said over his shoulder. "You fellas do for Frank what we did for Velma while me and Barney find your horses."

By the time Tucker came back leading the horses, the posse had buried Frank down the hill from Velma, out of eyesight if the shooter was waiting for another crack at them. The rocks piled atop Frank's body would do no more for him than they would for Velma: the coyotes or the wolves or the badgers would still paw the pile of stones until they got to the bodies. But it would give the men solace knowing they'd done what they could for them.

Tucker handed Ronnie his reins and walked to the fire. He squatted beside John lying on a blanket close to the heat. "How's the leg feel?" Tucker asked. "Can you still ride?"

John forced a smile. "Don't worry about me."

"You ought to be worried," Will said, looking up the hill as if he expected the Cauthers to come riding over. "We all ought to be worried." He refilled his coffee cup and replaced the pot on the coals. Ronnie had shot two grouse while Tucker was rounding up horses, and they hung over the flames. Tucker sliced off a leg dribbling fat onto the fire, flaring and spitting with every drip.

Will sat on a log across from Tucker and stared into the fire. "Somebody needs to get to a telegraph office. Wire the territorial marshal and tell him the Cauthers have thinned our ranks. Tell him we need help—"

"Just what did you expect?" Tucker said. He refilled John's

coffee cup before topping off his own. "Going after the Cauthers is a job for experienced men." He looked at Ronnie and Pasqual huddled together close to the fire. "What you need is a posse of gnarly bastards. Killers in their own right. Not these greenhorns."

"Maybe we ought to break off the trail," Ronnie said.

"I agree," Pasqual added. "With Frank dead"—he turned to Ronnie and put up his hands—"no offense. But with Frank gone, we got us another horse. Me and Ronnie could hightail it back to Ft. Pierre. Try to get help headed this way."

"They got a point," Will said.

Tucker shook his head. "A fine bunch of brave hearts you are. When we started out"—he nodded to Pasqual—"you couldn't get on the trail soon enough to get your money back. And you, Ronnie—as close as Frank was to you, you want to turn tail."

Ronnie nodded. "He *was* like a father to me. But before he died he told me he wanted to turn back—"

"I'll call bullshit on that," Tucker said. "Frank might not have been a gunny, but the man had sand. If he signed up to ride for this brand"—he motioned to Will—"he would have stuck with it."

"So now that Velma's dead, what's *your* reason for continuing?" Will asked.

"Yeah, mister scout," Pasqual pressed him, "just why do you want to find the Cauthers?"

Tucker had thought about that these last days. Did he always need a reason to see someone like Justice Cauther dangling from a rope? Or was it just the thrill of going after such dangerous game as a man with a rifle. "It's still about Velma. She was Jack's girl. But with her dead—especially in the way she was murdered—I want to catch them all the more now. I'm in it whether anyone's with me or not." He looked Will in the eyes.

"It's your call, Marshal."

Will kicked a rock with the toe of his boot. "We continue," he said after a long pause. "But someone's still got to go and wire a telegram to the territorial marshal."

"Tucker's right," Pasqual said. "If I go, I'll never see my money anyway."

"I lost more than Pasqual did," Ronnie said. "I lost a father in Frank and got more reason to see Justice Cauther dead. I can ride faster than he can anyway—"

"I'll go," John said, propping himself up on an elbow.

"You're in no shape to ride very far," Will said.

"I've had worse injuries than this," John said, holding out his hand. Tucker stood and hoisted him up. "I can ride out for Ft. Pierre and be there in two days. Besides, if I pass out, my Sadie will get me back to town just fine. She always has."

"Makes sense," Tucker said. "Ronnie and Pasqual can double up on Frank's sorrel."

"Then it's settled." Will handed John a half-eagle. "This will cover the wire. Tell them we need help bad."

John hobbled to his mare, and Tucker helped him into the saddle.

"Tie me," John said. "Just in case I pass out."

"See," Ronnie said. "The fat man ain't gonna' make it—"

"It's settled," Will said. "John's good for the ride. He damn sure wouldn't be good for a fight if we catch the Cauthers."

Tucker looked John over. He might just make it to wire for help if he didn't fall out of his saddle. "Give me some piggin' strings," Tucker told Ronnie.

"The hell I will."

Tucker's jaw clenched. He'd been on the trail four days with the likes of Ronnie, and he was reaching the end of his rope. He stepped closer. "Give me some now! You got some. Every damned cowboy's got piggin' strings to tie up nasty cows."

Ronnie backed away. He must have read something in Tucker he didn't like and reached into his saddlebags. He handed Tucker three leather strings, and Tucker lashed John to the saddle.

"Don't worry," John said. "Like I said, my Sadie will get me home."

Tucker watched John disappear over the next hill, riding toward Ft. Pierre, before stowing his coffee cup in his saddlebags. When he stepped into the stirrups, Will asked, "Where you going?"

Tucker drew his collar up against the stiff wind. "It'll be too slow with two men riding double. I was wrong about the gang hightailing it. They left that shooter behind to slow us down. Or stop us. With another man dead, and being slowed down with two men riding one horse, they'll figure for sure we have to give up. My guess is they're patting themselves on the back somewhere, taking a breather. And if I go on ahead, I figure to find them."

"What do we do?" Ronnie asked.

"Yeah," Will said. "Just what *do* we do? We're not exactly trackers."

"Even you'll be able to follow the trail I'll leave for you."

Chapter 12

Tucker spotted the soldiers riding the ridgeline nearly a mile away, perhaps thirty in a single file. If he saw them, then the Indians they searched for would have seen them, too. This patrol would be out a long time before they ever lucked on to any renegade Lakota. Perhaps, he thought, that was the intention of the commanding officer.

Tucker rode just below the ridgeline where the snow had blown clear, making riding easier, and intercepted the cavalry troop an hour later. They had stopped for their noon meal along Buzzard Creek, fed by the Bad River, what the Lakota called *Wakpa' Sica* for obvious reasons. The Bad, even in wet years, flowed at barely a trickle, just enough to stream its smelly, muddy waters to tributaries. Like the one the cavalry camped beside.

As he neared the camp, two flankers watched him warily, Spencers lying across their saddles. Tucker tied Barney to a clump of sage at the outer edge of the camp and walked in slowly. Soldiers knelt around three campfires, pots hanging over the flames, the smell of cooking salt pork and strong coffee perfuming the air. The soldiers watched him as he stopped beside a sergeant and an officer squatting beside a map laid on the ground.

The officer, a squat, heavyset man with mutton chops and bouncing jowls, stood and faced Tucker. "Tucker Ashley. My, my. Fancy seeing you here."

Tucker's jaw tightened when he recognized Abe Roush. He had been a lieutenant the last time Tucker and he had met. Back when Tucker knocked Roush on his keester for the third time over a bar girl who flirted with Tucker in the Bucket. He was scouting with the army then and earned himself a week in the guardhouse for striking an officer. "Captain now, I see. Congratulations."

The sergeant handed Roush a cup of coffee and held out another one for Tucker when Roush waved it away. "Tucker's not going to be in camp long enough to drink it." He smirked. "Just what do you want? I'm sure you didn't ride all the way out here just to congratulate me on my field promotion."

"I need help."

Captain Roush exaggerated looking Tucker up and down. "You look fine to me."

"It's the Cauther gang." Tucker explained they had murdered the saloon keeper in the Bucket of Blood and a roustabout before kidnapping and eventually murdering Velma Hart. And killing Frank this morning.

"And just what's that got to do with the U.S. Army?"

"We need help catching the Cauthers."

"A civilian matter?"

Tucker's jaw tightened further. He knew what was coming.

Roush smiled and waved his hand around the camp. "This patrol is tasked with finding those renegade Lakota."

Tucker started to speak, but Roush held up his hand. "We rode out of Ft. Abe Lincoln four days ago hunting Sioux who raided an Arikara camp along the upper Missouri, and I aim to find them. We can't become involved in civilian matters—"

"Last I knew, the army still wanted Justice Cauther."

Roush waved his hand at the surrounding rolling hills. "Like I said, all we got time for is looking for those Sioux."

"Then you're too far behind them." Tucker told Roush how

the posse had seen the raiding party leading the women hostages, and how they'd stolen two horses from them. He kept to himself the thought that the three remaining Sioux might be following Tucker because he freed their captives. "But that was two days ago. They could be out of the territory by now, selling their hostages, and you'd have wasted your time when you could be looking for Justice."

"And I'm to believe they stole horses and left that fine mule of yours?" Roush laughed and looked around. Soldiers seated around the nearest campfire laughed as well. "Guess those Indians wouldn't be caught dead riding that thing any more than the rest of us."

When Roush stopped laughing, he turned back to the map on the ground. "Now if there's nothing the army can do for you—"

"You got a farrier?"

"Of course," Roush said. "You know we always travel with one."

"My mule threw a shoe a couple miles back, and I'd like him to put a new one on."

"That's the least we can do for someone assisting the law. Donnely," Roush called over his shoulder.

Sgt. Donnely emerged from the back of a cavalry mount, a hook knife and hammer stuck in his leather apron. "Captain?"

"See that Ashley's mule gets a new shoe so he can ride the hell out of here."

Donnely walked to Tucker's mule and began examining Barney's hooves.

"Thought that was you," Tucker said. "Been two years."

"More like three," Donnely said and straightened. "Your mule don't have any shoes. Like most mules hereabouts."

"I know that." Tucker looked around the mule at Roush hunkered over the map. "But that damned fool don't."

"Then why—"

" 'Cause I thought you might help me."

Donnely jerked his thumb over his shoulder. "The captain's still pissed about that ass-whoppin' you gave him. If he caught me helping you—"

"It's important." Tucker lowered his voice.

Donnely bent beside Barney's leg. He grabbed a hoof knife and lifted it as if he were about to go to work. "What do you need?"

The soldiers had turned back to their fire and their noon meal and paid Donnely and Tucker no mind. "Is Jack Worman still out in the field?"

"He's out with Company C." Donnely took his hoof nippers from his apron as he glanced at Captain Roush, just out of earshot. "They're working toward the Wyoming line looking for those Sioux. We're due to rendezvous with them tomorrow."

"Then I need you to get word to Jack. Tell him I need help finding the Cauthers."

Donnely stood and shook his head. "I'll see what I can do, but don't count on it. The captain would have me shot if I helped you." He motioned to Roush. "Even the army is afraid of the Cauthers."

Tucker rode off a distance from the soldiers and dismounted. He stripped the saddle off Barney, and he swore the mule gave a sign of relief. "Just a quick break, my friend," Tucker said. He grabbed a clump of gramma grass and began rubbing the flanks, the withers, especially the mule's back where he'd carried the saddle almost every minute of the last few days.

Tucker grabbed a strip of buffalo jerky wrapped in an oilcloth and gnawed on the tough meat while he watched the cavalry patrol continue along the same ridge. They couldn't be more conspicuous if they'd fired off a volley of cannons. Perhaps that's just what Roush meant. And now he had Donnely to corroborate his feeling.

The only thing his foray into the army camp had gotten him was a "maybe" that Donnely would get word to Jack. Tucker needed him. Badly. The posse was somewhere miles behind him, making as good time as possible riding double. Roush offered no help, and the patrol had only managed to wipe out the Cauthers' trail leading right through where the cavalry had stopped for their noon meal.

And the Lakota. The four remaining warriors had ridden toward where the posse camped the night the Indians stole the horses. They would follow the posse and catch up sometime today. But what worried Tucker the most was that they would bypass the posse. Their vengeance wasn't against them. The Indians were such good trackers—ingrained from birth, almost—and would have recognized the tracks of the man who had sneaked into their camp, killed their friend, and freed their captives. They wouldn't risk a fight with the posse. They would come for the man riding the mule.

CHAPTER 13

Gall rode slowly into camp as if he had no cares in the world. Or had no worries that the posse followed him.

Justice stepped from behind a boulder. He leveled his gun at Gall until he recognized him. "Y'all sting them a little, did ya'?" Justice asked as Elias and Henny appeared from around the clump of rocks.

"More than a little," Gall answered and reached back into his saddlebags. He grabbed his tin cup and tossed it to Henny. "I need some coffee to warm me up."

"Get it yourself," Henny said.

Gall climbed down from his bay and stepped closer. "Don't think so. Without that woman to kick around, you got no other use around here."

Justice looked on with mild amusement as he studied Henny. He wondered what his half-brother would do; wondered if he'd stand up to Gall. He had his answer a moment later when Henny dropped his gaze and turned to the coffeepot.

Elias sat on a downed tree and pulled his mittens tighter. "I'm dying to know how badly you stung them."

"As am I," Justice said.

Henny walked toward Gall with the coffee cup, but Justice took it instead and began to sip. He'd tolerate Gall coming down on Henny, but only so much. Gall sometimes thought he called the shots. Justice had to remind him now and again he was wrong. "Is the posse going to be a problem anymore?"

Gall glared at his cup in Justice's hand but said nothing about it. "I drilled that old bow-legged guy, the one that hobbled around like he had a cob up his keester. Scattered the horses, too."

"The cowboy! How about Ashley?" Justice said. "Did you drill him or not?"

"I made him dive for cover like the rest."

"But you didn't hit him?"

Gall shrugged. "Can't say for sure, but I sent a few slugs down his way. Even if they find their critters, it'll be days before they can regroup. My best guess is we got nothing to worry about from them."

"Good," Justice said and handed Gall his coffee cup.

"Don't be so smug just yet." Gall finished the coffee and tossed the grounds lying in the bottom to one side of the fire. "When I was lying there, waiting for the posse, a cavalry patrol passed. I watched for a while when they camped by Buzzard Creek. They was looking mighty hard—"

"For Indians, no doubt," Elias said. "Remember that scalped Sioux we saw a couple days ago, the one the posse killed?"

"We can't assume the army is looking just for them," Justice said. He squatted by the fire and grabbed a twig from the pile. "Draw where the cavalry rode. The terrain."

Gall bent to one knee and drew in the snow the ridgeline the cavalry rode, up until the time they camped.

"So, they rode high?"

Gall nodded.

"Crap!" Justice said. "If they're looking for Indians, they sure won't find them like that. They gotta be looking for us."

"Not likely," Henny volunteered, as if his opinion mattered. "The army doesn't involve itself with civilian matters."

Justice often felt like slapping his half-wit brother senseless. This was one of those times. "Out here," Justice said, "the army is often the *only* law there is. Which direction were they headed?"

Gall drew a line pointing southwest. "They headed into Hellion. Probably to let off a little steam."

Justice kicked snow over the fire and turned toward the hamlet of Hellion. "We need to find out if they're hunting us." He faced Elias—the only one of them with common enough features to blend in—just another farmer going about his business. Whenever the gang needed to scout a job somewhere in a town, Elias was always the one to go. And he enjoyed it. That he returned often dotted with blood from a fresh kill from his town foray mattered not to Justice. As long as Elias brought the information back. With no one the wiser that the balding man in bib overalls and thick Norwegian accent was a killer without conscience. "Ride into town and buy those soldiers some drinks to loosen their lips. Find out if we're on their bunting list."

Elias smiled and grabbed his saddle blanket from atop his saddle. He shook the dusting of snow off before laying it on his gelding's back. Justice looked at him from the other side of the horse. "And take Henny with you."

"What?!"

"You heard right," Justice said. "Take the kid with you."

"What the hell for?"

"He's got to learn the ins and out of the business sometime."

"I am no vet nurse—"

"Just do it," Justice said. "Give the kid something to do—hold on to the horses or something. But keep him out of sight—his description is on the Wanted posters, too."

"You going to be here ven I come back?"

Justice chin-pointed to the west. "As much as I'd like to think Gall discouraged the posse from following, there's still the joker in the deck—Tucker Ashley. Horse or no, if he's able, he'll still be on our trail. Gall and me will wait up this side of the Swede's ranch. Now hightail it to town and meet us in that box canyon yonder."

As Elias threw his leg over the saddle, Justice stopped him. "And for once, don't kill anyone you don't need to. Last thing we need is more attention to us."

Elias winked. "You know that everyone I kill, I haf to."

Chapter 14

The trail abruptly stopped, as if every one of the Cauther gang had grown wings and taken flight. If this was the woods, Tucker would continually scan the trees. Many men he fought with failed to look up. And many were killed by an overhead ambush. But here on the prairie, there was nothing above but heavy snow clouds, and the sun fighting those clouds to peek through.

Tucker spent the afternoon looking for the gang's trail after the army destroyed it in passing. But when he spotted the Cauthers' hastily broken camp a mile back, tracking them had been easy. They had made no attempt to hide their trail—riding through snow-covered sagebrush and scrub juniper with broken branches betraying their direction.

But now? As he walked bent over, studying the ground, he kept looking around for places for an ambush. He recalled how easily he had been lulled before into thinking the Cauthers had lit out after that first ambush; how they made no effort to hide their trail because they were on the run. But now? "Where the hell could they have gone?"

Barney's ears twitched as if he were mulling over the question, and he gave a faint snort.

"You're no help," Tucker said and resumed studying the ground. The gang had begun hiding their trail two miles back. Tracking them over this frozen earth, with the wind blowing the snow free, was like tracking them over granite: all one could hope for was an occasional scuff of a hoof, or an overturned rock, or a broken branch. They had even stopped to pick up horse apples when their mounts dropped, denying Tucker both a confirmation of direction and a clue as to how the horses were eating and from where. With the gang taking great pains to hide their trail, Tucker had lost them. There was a reason few posses ever caught Justice Cauther—he was just too wily at hiding his trail.

Light snow had begun the last hour, falling straight down when the wind stopped. Tucker knew if he didn't pick up their trail soon, his chances of finding the gang were even more remote.

He mounted the mule and rode out in a lazy semicircle from where he was. Why had they suddenly decided to hide their tracks? Was it to confound the posse if they followed, or was there another reason? Were they planning another raid somewhere and needed to be doubly careful in case the posse regrouped? Tucker doubted that. Will's raggedy bunch had been thoroughly shaken by Frank's murder. They jumped at every noise of a hawk or meadowlark, every gust of wind that rolled a Russian thistle across the prairie. Tucker had no illusions: he knew what was left of Will's posse would be little help. The only help he could count on was from Jack Worman. If he could find him and lure him away from scouting for the army.

The sun peeked from the clouds for a moment, and Tucker bent low over the saddle. With John shot to hell and Frank dead—and with two horses lost to the Indians—Tucker had been tempted to agree to let the others to turn back. Velma's murder made the journey personal, but he warned himself to be cautious: a man who took things personally made mistakes. And he dared make none with Justice Cauther.

He kept his eyes looking into the sun when . . . a broken cactus stem stood out among the clump of plants spread across the ground. Tucker dismounted and bent to the stem, browned where something had passed and snapped it. It could have been a mountain sheep or a buffalo that still roamed this part of the territory. Or it could have been caused by the Cauthers riding through.

He brushed light snow from the ground, working in a loose arc, when the scuff he'd prayed for showed itself: a scuff from a horse's hoof.

He estimated the stride of the animal and spotted a deeper hoof print where the rider had spurred his horse across a shallow coulee. He ran his hand over the indentation. He recognized it from that first day he got on to the trail of the Cauthers. One of the gang rode a horse with a pronounced chunk missing from one hoof. A good farrier, like Sgt. Donnely, could correct it. But when you were on the run constantly like the Cauthers, visiting a farrier was the last luxury on your mind. You were more likely to run an animal into the ground and steal another than risk getting help for the horse.

Tucker walked several paces farther along until he picked up another hoof scuff: he now knew the direction of travel. But this print was no different from the others he had seen trailing the gang. Except this horse rode alongside the horse with the cracked hoof. And they rode toward Hellion.

From long distance through binoculars, Hellion was one of those little sleepy-appearing burgs that had sprung up—illegally—on Sioux land. It boasted a livery and general store that sat beside what once had been a church. The steeple thrust its tired spire heavenward, fooling travelers passing by that Hellion was actually civilized enough to have a church. Its last preacher was buried out back. The town was just large enough to afford an unofficial town marshal, and one saloon.

But it was known as the wildest place this side of Ft. Pierre, where a man could get anything he wanted. And much of what he didn't bargain for, as the crowded cemetery beside the last preacher could attest to. Tucker had been to Hellion some years ago and had to kill a man there when he tried stealing Tucker's mule. And though he had no desire to go into town, he knew he must follow the horse with the cracked hoof.

He stowed the binoculars and rode slowly into town, the cracked-hoof prints disappearing among all the other hoof prints clogging the fetid street. Clustered around the saloon were horses tied to rails, steam rising from impatient nostrils, from horse droppings on the frozen street, from the stench of urine. Tucker eased his mule warily past the saloon. The man who rode the horse with the bad hoof was here in town somewhere—: in the saloon or in the shadows. Somewhere. Would he know Tucker on sight? He had to assume that Justice—or whoever rode the Cauther horse—would know him from the ambush that wounded John. Tucker scanned the tops of the buildings and the dark shadows between them on his way to the town marshal's office. A lamp lit the office, and Tucker dismounted. A note had been tacked to the door with a fence staple:

GONE TO MAYBELLINE'S SALOON. LAST TABLE IN BACK.

Tucker walked Barney toward the saloon and coaxed him past two range mustangs stomping the dirt as they tried pulling away from the reins. On the other side must have been every mount that B Company of the 7th Cavalry rode, taking up most of the street. Tucker nudged Barney between two cavalry mounts and looped the reins over the hitching post.

He paused at the door to the saloon and peeked through the glass. What would the two Cauthers look like? He had a faint description from the Wanted posters—at least those gang members known to the Pinkertons—but he had never met any of them. Were they interspersed with the soldiers clustered around the roulette table losing their meager monthly wages, or placing bets at a poker table they'd never win from the rigged house? Or were they indulging in another vice? One soldier staggered down the stairs. He slipped his arms through his suspenders and pulled them tight over his shoulders while another walked past him arm-in-arm with a whore on the way to her upstairs crib.

Tucker spotted Captain Roush seated with two cowboys playing poker at a table in back of the saloon. A painted lady sat on his lap kissing his neck and rubbing his muttonchops with one hand while the other one slipped inside his shirt pocket. She came away with gold coins and slipped them in a pouch strapped to her thigh.

The dealer—younger than Tucker but a dandy, with his silk vest and polished boots—wore a star, and his pistol hung close to his vest in a shoulder rig. One of the cowboys said something, and the marshal said something in return that Tucker could not hear over the din of the drunks, but their looks suggested someone had been caught cheating. Or was suspected of it.

He paused before entering, looking over the crowd once more. But even Tucker could not put a face to a man based on a hoof print. He hoped someone inside had seen the Cauthers ride into town.

When he opened the door, warmth washed over him from the enormous pot-bellied stove in one corner of the saloon. He picked his way through soldiers and cowboys and leaned against the bar. The bardog—wide and rangy with the knuckles of a man who'd bartended rough saloons all his life—pulled on the handlebar mustache sitting under his misshapen nose. A dirty flour sack towel was slung over his shoulder, and he picked up a stub of a cigar from an ashtray. "We got warm beer," he said as he chewed on his cigar, "and rotgut that would deworm a flock of sheep. That's the choices."

"I don't have worms," Tucker said. "So I'll have the beer."

"Wise choice." The bardog turned to a spigot and tapped beer into a chipped mug. Tucker struggled to spot the beer, the mug seeming to be filled only with foam the color of stale urine. "Two bits."

Tucker fished into his vest pocket, and flipped money on to the bar. "Kind of pricy, but if you can give me some information, it'll be worth it."

The bartender leaned against the bar back and grabbed a glass. He yawned on it before polishing it with his towel. "What kind of information?" he asked as he stacked the glass atop others under the broken mirror.

"Looking for men—"

He held up his hands as if in surrender. "Can't help you there, pard'ner. Now if you're looking for some women—"

"Not looking for men for *that,*" Tucker said. "Men I'm looking for came in here within the last couple hours I'd reckon."

"Why didn't you say so?" The man laughed as he waved his arm around the saloon. "All these soldier boys came in within the last couple hours."

"Not soldiers I'm looking for."

"You a bounty hunter?" the bartender asked.

"Not today."

"Can't help you, pard'ner." He pointed to the table in back of the room. "Talk to Marshal Olsen over there." He leaned across the bar and lowered his voice. "But I'd wait until he's winning. When he's losing like he has been, he can be a real horse's patoot."

A soldier at the far end of the bar yelled at the bardog, leaving Tucker sandwiched between two soldiers. They looked him over pie-eyed before returning to their whisky.

"Soldiers can't haf much of a conversation." A man in the bib overalls and denim coat of a farmer slid between the soldiers. He sucked on a licorice stick as he stood with his back to the bar looking over the rowdies. "Wonder what brings these soldier boys to these parts?" he asked in a thick Scandinavian accent.

"Hunting Lakota'd be my guess," Tucker answered.

The man laughed heartily. "Why else would soldiers be in this jerkwater town in the middle of the territory?" He downed his beer and held up his mug for another. "What brings *you* here?" He nodded upstairs. "Maybe you need a woman? I just visited a real sweetheart—"

"Don't need a woman. I'm hunting two men."

"What men?"

Tucker was reluctant to say any more than necessary. It was his cautious nature, he supposed. "Just some men who rode into town a couple hours ago. One of the horses cut its hoof sometime in the last few days." He eyed the farmer suspiciously. "When did you ride into Hellion?"

The man looked at the ceiling as if the answer was scribbled there among the bullet holes. "Yesterday about noon. And I am afraid I cannot help you any." He pointed to the poker table. "But the marshal there is winning, so he might know these men you look for."

Tucker finished his mug of foam and headed for the poker table. "Thanks, friend," he said over his shoulder as the man adjusted the suspenders of his bib overalls. Like most farmers do dozens of times a day.

Chapter 15

Tucker walked through soldiers standing off to one side betting on one of theirs, who was arm wrestling a cowboy. The soldier grunted, and his arm shook, while the cowboy—twice the soldier's age and showing but one tooth—smiled and held his arm immobile. He winked at the soldier and put his arm on the table. "My half eagle," he said, and the soldier reluctantly flipped the money to him.

Tucker stopped at the poker table and looked down at Marshal Olsen. He turned his cards over to reveal a straight flush, and Tucker was tempted to tell the cowboys across the table that the good marshal had slipped that red king he needed from inside his vest. The cowboy—too broke to continue playing—knocked his chair over as he left the game.

Olsen raked in his pot, while the whore bouncing on his lap planted a lip lock on him and giggled. The marshal grabbed a gold dollar and tucked it down her bosom. He looked up at Tucker, as if seeing him for the first time. "You need something?" He nodded to an empty chair vacated by the cowboy. "We suddenly got us an opening."

"Not for him," Roush said. "This one is just passing through, ain't you, Ashley?"

"As soon as I get some help from the marshal here."

"Help with what?" Olsen asked.

Roush downed his whisky and yelled for another glass. "Ashley here wants help finding the Cauther gang."

Olsen choked on his beer. "That right?" The marshal eyed him. "You want me to help you fight the Cauthers?"

Tucker nodded. "I tracked two of them into town. They weren't more than an hour ahead of me."

Olsen looked frantically around the saloon, and his hand rested on his gun butt in the fancy shoulder rig. "What do they look like?"

"Never saw them," Tucker said. "But I thought you might have noticed a couple men who rode into town recently—"

Marshal Olsen belly-laughed, the painted lady on his lap bouncing with him. He wiped beer off his chin as he waved around the saloon. "Between Roush's boys getting liquored up and the cowboys and drifters figuring they're tougher than the soldiers, fights have been non-stop, and it's all I can do to keep on top of things. The town folks—if you consider the owner of the saloon and the livery—pay me for keeping the peace right here. They don't pay me to go after killers, especially the likes of the Cauther gang."

"Sure, Marshal." Tucker nodded to Olsen's cards. "By the looks of it, you're working overtime enforcing the laws here."

Olsen's smile faded. "I don't like your tone—"

"And I don't particularly like some fat-assed marshal refusing to help find a gang of killers."

Olsen shoved the woman off his lap. She plopped onto the floor unceremoniously, and her petticoat rode up over her legs.

Olsen stood, and he took a step back. His hand hovered around his gun butt sticking out of the shoulder holster, some tiny nickel-plated affair Tucker thought went well with the dandy's attire.

"I wouldn't pull that little gun," Tucker warned.

"He's right," Roush said. "This one is as bad as the Cauthers. You wouldn't see daylight through that holster before he'd drop you."

Olsen was drunk, but not drunk enough to have lost all his senses. He seemed to mull over his chances and finally dropped his hand to his side. "Get the hell away from my table. You want men to join your posse, feel free to recruit any able-bodied drunk in the place. Now scat!"

Tucker kept Marshal Olsen in his periphery as he turned and picked his way through the crowd of rowdy soldiers and cowboys. He spotted a few gunnies among the drunks, easily identified by the cut-down holsters, the notches crudely carved on grips. Rigs worn by men in Justice Cauther's business. Olsen was right—he'd find no help among these fools. And any of the gunnies could be the men he trailed here.

He looked a final time around the saloon floor, at a soldier playing mumblety-peg in stocking feet with a cowboy who'd stripped his boots off as well, while men cheered and bet on the throw of the knife. An NCO poured whisky down a young private's throat while he was held by two others, and Tucker sidestepped two range-weary men fighting in one corner of the saloon. The Cauthers might be among these men; he just had no way of knowing.

Tucker was headed for the door when two soldiers stepped in front of him and blocked his path. Tucker started around the one—a sergeant fully a head taller than Tucker and forty pounds heavier—when the man put a mitt on Tucker's chest and shoved him back. He nearly tripped over a chair but regained his balance when the smaller of the two—a private with kinky, red hair—moved to flank him. One of the soldier's cheekbones had healed wrong at one time and lay flatter than the other, while old scars above his eyes told Tucker this one was a scrapper. "I'm thinking your attitude needs changed."

Tucker moved to face both men, but the private kept moving behind Tucker, forcing him to divide his attention between them. "I don't follow you."

"Man said you were flapping your gums, saying how we couldn't find Indians if they were sitting on the ground waiting for us." He had slipped his galluses off and left them dangling beside his waist.

"I don't recall that conversation," Tucker said.

"I don't figure the guy would lie about it," the private said. He moved to Tucker's back so that he had a difficult time keeping both soldiers in sight.

"What guy?' Tucker said, pivoting to keep the small man in his sight. He'd be the quick one. And he'd be the one to spot any weakness.

"That farmer who was just here." The sergeant stepped closer. "The one who just rode in ahead of you."

"The guy with the bib overalls?" Tucker looked around the crowd. They'd stopped their drinking and gambling. They smelled blood, and they were sure it would be Tucker's that got spilled. One soldier moved a table out of the middle of the floor, and a cowboy shoved chairs aside. The crowd formed a circle around the three, and bets began being exchanged among them.

The big man stepped closer, but Tucker moved just out of his reach, putting a table between himself and the sergeant. Tucker looked around the crowd, but there wasn't a friendly face to be seen. All they wanted was to watch the next customer get ready for the cemetery in back of the church.

The sergeant tossed the table aside, and it crashed, splintering into the door.

"I don't have time for this," Tucker said as he moved away when . . .

The private moved in quickly and lashed out with a stiff jab that caught Tucker flush on the cheek. He staggered back, amazed at the ferocity of the blow from such a small feller.

Tucker was struggling to regain his balance when the private threw a right cross. Tucker jerked his head back, and the blow glanced off his head as he caught sight of the sergeant moving to Tucker's back, circling behind him.

"Sergeant Harris!" Roush called out, and the big man stopped to look at his commander. "Have fun," Roush winked. "But don't get too rambunctious."

The sergeant grinned and stepped toward Tucker. He swung a clumsy roundhouse that Tucker easily ducked.

But not the blow the scrapper threw that landed on Tucker's temple. He went down to the floor and looked up just as the sergeant reared back and kicked Tucker in the pit of his stomach. The air *whooshed* out of him, and he sucked in great gulps of air as he held his stomach.

The sergeant laughed only slightly less than Captain Roush and Marshal Olsen as Tucker used a chair to clamber to his feet. The sergeant slapped Tucker back to the floor and straddled him. He rested his hands on his knees as he accepted a beer from another soldier watching the night's entertainment. "See, we don't cotton to civilians spreading lies about our outfit. Call it pride. We are quite capable of finding them Sioux—"

Tucker was clawing at the chair to regain his footing, when he spotted an opening. As Sergeant Harris blew foam off the mug and downed his beer, Tucker grabbed a spittoon within reach beside a table. He dipped his shoulder, picked out a spot on the sergeant's chin, and clutched the brass pot.

He swung it for all he was worth. The blow landed on the big man's chin, and his eyes rolled back in his head before he fell backwards on the floor. His legs kicked once and stopped, and Tucker wondered if he'd killed the man. Which would have been a bonus, the way he felt.

The private looked in astonishment at his partner lying immobile on the floor. Tucker used the chair to help stand. He stood on wobbly legs only momentarily before he rushed the private.

He backed up into the crowd.

A cowboy shoved the private back onto the middle of the floor and right into Tucker's uppercut. The private's head snapped back, and he sank to one knee. Tucker bent down and backhanded him, and he toppled to the floor.

The jeering soldiers watching the fight grew silent, none stopping Tucker as he picked up his hat and started for the door after the farmer. He'd stepped around the private when he heard the man stand. When Tucker turned toward the sound, the private had drawn an Arkansas toothpick and waved the air with it. "We don't appreciate you making monkeys of us. I think I'll slice off a chunk of your liver before the night's done."

"I don't see it that way," Tucker said as he drew his pistol. He pointed it at the private's chest and cocked the hammer. "I don't have time to fight fair."

"I figure you got all the time in the world," Marshal Olsen said as he jammed his gun barrel in Tucker's ribs. "Drop that gun of yours. I don't allow no lopsided fight here in Hellion. Go on, drop it."

Tucker let his gun drop to the floor. "And him with a knife isn't lopsided?"

"Let's say troublemakers like you play the hand they're dealt," Olsen said. "But if it was me, I'd formulate a plan real quick-like. Captain Roush says that little private Clegg is mighty handy with a blade."

With the fight back on, soldiers elbowed cowboys as they whooped and hollered. They jockeyed for a good view of the spectacle. They made a tight circle around Tucker and the private, and bets passed between drunken men. Private Clegg smiled wickedly as he slashed the air with his knife, a preview of what he had in mind. He suddenly feinted right, then border-shifted the knife to his left hand and lashed out. Tucker sucked in his stomach, but the blade cut through his coat and dug a shallow furrow across his gut. "How's it feel, big man?" Clegg said, grinning. "That's for hurting my sergeant," he said as he circled to Tucker's right.

The private lunged forward and jabbed twice with the knife. Tucker dodged the first thrust, but not the second as the blade cut through his coat and sliced his shoulder. Sticky blood seeped onto his shirt, and the crowd roared their approval.

Another soldier handed the private a mug of beer, and he took a long pull before tossing it aside. He began circling Tucker, flicking out the knife, teasing.

Tucker backed up, and his hand came to rest on a whisky bottle atop a table. He grabbed it and smashed it just as the private moved in. Tucker thrust the broken bottle at the man's head.

It sliced a nasty furrow across one eye and down the side of his cheek.

Blood dripped into his eye.

He yelled and dropped his blade.

Tucker stepped toward him as . . .

Another soldier stuck out his leg, and Tucker tripped over it. He fell sprawling to the floor and hit his cheek on a chair.

He struggled to stand as the private found his knife lying beside a spittoon. He wiped blood out of his eye, from his cheek.

Clegg circled to Tucker's side, and Tucker tried keeping the private in his sight.

The private feinted a slash, then lunged at Tucker's midsection.

Tucker backpedaled.

The private moved in for the killing thrust. Blood lust ran loud, and the crowd yelled their approval.

Tucker backed into a chair, and his hand closed on one leg.

Clegg lunged.

Tucker swung the chair and caught the private on both knees. The sound of breaking bones was loud even over the crowd, and everyone instantly became silent as the private, howling in pain, dropped his knife onto the floor. Tucker swung the chair again, and it crashed over the private's head, knocking him unconscious.

Tucker shuffled to a table to help him stand, but his shoulder gave out, and he fell back to the floor. When he tried using his good arm, he heard Marshal Olsen behind him. He leveled his gun at Tucker and said through teeth clenched in rabid rage, "You son of a bitch," and cocked his Colt. "I keep a peaceful town . . ."

Tucker's gun lay across the room. "Try it," Olsen said.

The gun was too far. The marshal had the drop on him. But the private's knife was only inches away from his grasp.

Tucker snatched the toothpick, and swung it in a tight arc before the drunken marshal could react. He drove it through Olsen's boot, impaling his foot to the floor. Olsen dropped his gun and screamed while he pulled frantically at the knife. Cowboys laughed. Soldiers looked on with interest. No one made an effort to help the marshal.

Captain Roush came off the chair, and threw his whore aside. He clawed at his pistol, but Tucker snatched Olsen's from the floor first. Before Roush could clear his holster, Tucker had aimed the marshal's gun at the captain and cocked the hammer. The drunk soldiers didn't help their commanding officer any more than they'd helped Marshal Olsen, and fresh bets were whispered around the crowd. "Leave it holstered, Roush."

"You'll be shot for this, Ashley."

Tucker waved the gun around the saloon. The cowboys and soldiers had grown quiet, and they backed away from Tucker. They watched Roush to see what he would do—the only noise

Olsen's wailing as he tried dislodging the knife from his foot. "Even if your men were sober enough to remember what happened, do you think any court in the territory would convict me for defending myself? Especially after you gave your boys a wink and a nod."

"I'll see you hang."

"But not tonight." Tucker stepped toward Roush. He snatched Roush's gun from the holster and tucked it into his waistband. He ignored Olsen's screams of pain as he retrieved his own gun and holstered it. "Same goes for you, Marshal. You make an issue of this, and I'll see to it the territorial marshal pays you a visit."

Olsen, blood seeping out of his boot, writhed on the floor, with cowboys and soldiers and gunnies looking on with amusement.

"Your gun will be in the horse trough when you get your sorry ass unstuck," Tucker said as he backed out the door. "Yours too, Captain."

Tucker backed out the door and ran into the night. One of the Cauthers—dressed like a farmer—had left the saloon moments before the soldiers jumped Tucker. And Tucker was bent on finding him.

CHAPTER 16

Tucker ran out the door, and frigid air washed his sweat-drenched face. He slipped into the space between the saloon and the livery and stood motionless. Watching the street. Letting his eyes adapt to the darkness. The farmer was out here somewhere, perhaps waiting for Tucker to make a mistake. In their brief meeting earlier, Tucker recalled how thick the man was in the arms and shoulders, just like a working man. He'd be a handful in a fair fight, especially with Tucker's cut shoulder. But if the man rode with Justice Cauther, he wouldn't make it a fair fight. And neither would Tucker if he got the chance.

Three cowboys stopped in front of the saloon and wedged their horses between cavalry mounts. They looked his way, but couldn't see him in the shadows and swaggered inside.

When Tucker caught his breath, he stuffed his bandana under his shirt. Private Clegg's Arkansas toothpick had sliced his shoulder muscle and nicked a spurter. The cold air felt good, relieving some of the pain, and the bandana stopped the flow of blood for now.

Inside the saloon, the screams of pain from Marshal Olsen rose above the din of the drunks, and Tucker imagined that no one as yet helped the marshal. Tucker expected Roush to rush outside with some of his troopers in pursuit, but they hadn't. Drunk soldiers don't obey orders very well, as Tucker recalled from his days in the war.

With the three cowboys inside the saloon, the street stood

empty, and Tucker left the safety of the shadows. The farmer and another of the Cauthers had ridden into town just before Tucker had, and one of them owned a horse with a nicked hoof. Tucker recalled seeing two distinct sets of tracks. If the farmer was still here, his companion might be as well.

Tucker began looking at the horses tied in front of the saloon, backing up to each one and lifting legs, checking for the telltale hoof print. He bypassed the cavalry mounts and horses of the cowboys who'd just ridden in and went to each of the other cowboy mounts in turn. Time was not his friend: the Cauther with the horse might already be out of town.

He looked at a dozen horses and was bent over another, checking a hoof, when he felt—just *felt*—someone behind him. He smelled licorice, and he straightened up just as someone behind him said, "I like to see the man's face I kill," in a thick Norwegian accent. "Shof your hands deep into your pockets and turn around."

Tucker stuck his hands in his pockets before he turned slowly around. The farmer stood a dozen feet in front of Tucker, holding a Smith and Wesson .44 in one hand and a licorice stick in the other. He smiled as he sucked on the candy, and Tucker fought the urge to rip his hands from his pockets and go for broke. But that was like putting a bullet to his head himself, and he needed to stall and figure out how to reach his Remington on his belt. "You buy that candy from Moore's Mercantile?"

The man grinned a wide smile missing the front teeth. "You do remember."

"Are you at least going to give me a name before you ventilate me?"

The farmer sucked on the licorice stick. His gun barrel moved from Tucker's head to his chest. "Elias Gates."

"Ah," Tucker said, slowly wiggling his hands out of his

pockets. "You're the one who rides with Justice Cauther that no one can identify."

Elias shrugged. "Guess I am just too common."

"Guess so," Tucker said, his hands inching out of his pockets. "Only thing people remember about you is that you're a back shooter. You sure you don't want me to turn around so you can drill me in the back?"

"You son hof a bitch," Elias said.

His arm stretched out.

He cocked his gun.

Things slowed for Tucker then. Elias's trigger finger whitened as it applied pressure, and Tucker knew he couldn't get his hands out of his pockets before . . .

"What brains you have is gonna' be splattered all over the street if you don't lower that hogleg." Sgt. Donnely jammed the barrel of his government Colt into the back of Elias's head.

A look of indecision crossed Elias's face.

"Holster it!" Donnely ordered.

Elias did as he was told and turned his head to look at Donnely. "You're going to regret this—"

"That remains to be seen," the sergeant said. His gun remained centered on Elias's head as he backed away. "You can take your hands out of your pockets, Tucker."

Tucker did so, and he worked the stiffness out of his gun hand. He'd hit the big soldier in the saloon hard enough to bust a knuckle, and his hand was stiffening quickly in the cold.

Donnely backed up farther, and Elias looked from him to Tucker, weighing his options. "*Now,* Mr. Farmer, we can have us a fair fight." Donnely holstered his gun but left the holster flap untied. Just in case.

Elias put up his hands. "I do not vant any trouble," he told Tucker and turned to leave.

Then he quickly dropped to one knee and drew his .44 as he

spun around and faced Tucker. His gun had cleared the holster when . . .

Tucker's first bullet struck Elias center chest. Before he fell, Tucker's second round entered Elias's eye socket, and the man was dead before he toppled over.

Cowboys poured from the saloon to see what the gunplay was about. Tucker hastily thumbed fresh cartridges into his gun. He kicked Elias's gun aside and glared at the crowd, but none of the drunks confronted him. All they wanted was to see the results of the gunplay.

"I owe you, Donnely."

Sgt. Donnely kept an eye on the crowd as it slowly filtered back inside the saloon. "It's me who owes you. After Captain Roush ordered those two soldiers to rough you up, I got plumb ashamed."

The crescendo of the crowd rose inside, and Tucker could make out voices calling for his death. "The marshal finally got his foot unstuck." Donnely cocked an ear. "I came out to warn you Roush fired up the troops when I seen this peckerwood." He nodded to the corpse. "My guess is they're just now recovering from their shock of two of their own beaten right under their noses. Won't be but a few minutes, and they'll bail out of the saloon after you with blood on their minds."

Donnely stepped closer and lowered his voice. "But I'll make it up to you. We're to rendezvous with Company C tomorrow. Jack Worman's with them, and I'll give him the word. Where should he meet you?"

"Aren't you afraid your unit won't find the Lakota if you lose your best scout?"

Donnely chuckled, keeping watch on the last of the crowd that had filtered back into Maybelline's. "With that buffoon Roush in charge of both companies, we won't even come across a cold Indian campfire."

Tucker waited until the last rowdy shut the saloon door before he answered. "I'm not sure where I'll be. Elias here rode into town with another of the Cauthers—"

"What the hell's going on here?" The livery man came out of his sleeping room inside the barn, rubbing his eyes and scratching his crotch. His red flannel underwear reminded Tucker of John's underthings. Except not so pretty. "What the hell's the commotion . . ." He stopped when he nearly tripped over Elias's body. "I see this is the corpse of the day. Shame."

"What's a shame?" Tucker asked.

The livery man kicked Elias's boot. "This one seemed like a nice feller. Not like his partner."

"What partner?"

"Some kid who rode into town with him." The livery man spat tobacco juice, and it splatted against Elias's bloody head. "Some pimply faced kid. Maybe twenty, twenty-one. He had a real slow manner about him, like that inbred bastard I had working for me couple years ago. But this kid had an attitude. Real nasty he was. I told him he needed to trim his bay's hoof—it had a nasty chunk out of it—and he threatened to ventilate me if I didn't mind my own business."

"Recognize him?" Donnely asked Tucker.

"Henny Cauther."

The livery man slumped. "No one said the Cauthers was in town—"

"Where's the kid now?"

The livery man trembled, and Tucker reached over and slapped his arm. "Where?"

"There," he pointed northwest. "Kid rode out thataway. When I heard the shootin', I woke up and seen the kid in the livery waiting for the farmer. He lit out, never even waiting to see if the farmer was alive."

"What's to the northwest?" Tucker asked.

"There's a narrow spot in the White River. That would be the logical place for the kid to ride. But he won't get far," the livery man said, stuffing more tobacco in his cheek. "The White's awfully alkaline."

Tucker had ridden land such as this, desert land with little rainfall, where the only water available was alkali springs. Tucker had to boil the water before he could drink it, but horses weren't so lucky. Tucker would keep Barney from an alkaline spring, but kept away from any water too long, the mule could get colic.

"But the Swede's ranch is thataway," Donnely said. "Only place I can think of he'd be able to get any fresh water. Old man Lundgren has a pretty decent spread on the far side of the White. He charges the army to drink from his pond but don't charge most folks. That'd be the logical way for the kid to ride if he was to meet up with his gang."

"Then I'll head toward the Swede's ranch." Tucker faced Donnely. "Tell Jack to find my posse—they're wandering somewhere around Silver Springs—and lead them to the Swede's ranch. Sounds like the only place Justice could hole up and wait for Elias and his brother." He looked at Elias's corpse still littering the street. "And Elias *is* going to be a little late."

Sergeant Harris burst from the saloon holding the side of his head, followed by three more soldiers rushing to get out. They spotted Tucker and staggered toward him, drawing their pistols as they ran. "Get your butt out of here," Donnely said. "In no time, the whole company will be after you."

"Thanks." Tucker swung a leg over the mule. "By the way, who does Roush have tracking for him?"

"Dilly McMasters is meeting us here in the morning," Donnely said. "And he's mighty good."

"I know," Tucker said and spurred Barney.

The mule seemed to realize the danger, and he leapt forward

just as shots erupted. One bullet cut his ear as it whizzed by. The rest of the drunken soldiers' bullets went far astray. *But not for long,* Tucker thought. With Dilly McMasters tracking, it was just a matter of time before they'd be on his trail.

Chapter 17

Tucker easily picked up the track of the horse with the bad hoof. The rider—Henny Cauther, if the description of the livery man was correct—made no attempt to hide his tracks but galloped hard and fast over frozen ground. That his horse maintained its footing was a testament to the horseflesh. No doubt stolen.

Henny didn't worry Tucker. He had no trail sense like his brother, and Tucker knew he'd be able to follow the kid wherever he fled. What worried him were the fifteen soldiers led by little Dilly McMasters. Tucker had ridden with the tiny Scotsman two summers ago when they both scouted for the 7th out of Ft. Abe Lincoln. Dilly—son of a Scottish river man and a Crow mother—had been raised by his mother's people while his father floated the upper Missouri. Dilly had picked up the trail savvy of the Crow, and the army put his instincts to good use. Jack Worman was a superb scout, Tucker a mite better at reading sign. But Dilly saw things that weren't there. Local legend claimed Dilly could track a raccoon across a river, but that had never been proved.

Still, he was the last man Tucker wanted to lead an army platoon bent on catching and killing him. Especially since Dilly thought he had a score to settle with Tucker. That year Tucker and Dilly scouted together, Dilly had gotten drunk. Insulted every man in the company. But he took a special interest in Tucker, finally pulling a knife on Tucker when he wouldn't rile up. Tucker had heard the stories about Dilly's ability with a blade—he'd never lost a knife fight, it was rumored—and he had no desire to prove them wrong that night. So, when Tucker drew his gun and threatened to kill Dilly, he'd sworn one day to catch Tucker without his pistol.

Tucker stopped in a bunch of tall gramma grass and dropped the reins. Barney began munching on the grass, while Tucker dismounted and stretched. He grabbed his binoculars and watched his back trail. He spotted the soldiers—just minute specks in his binoculars—riding steadily, not hard like sober men can, but steady enough as they followed Dilly single file. In another couple hours, the booze would have been all puked out of their gullets, and they could ride harder and push the limit in their search for Tucker.

Tucker grabbed a chunk of jerky and chewed on it as he looked through the binoculars again. Behind Dilly rode Sergeant Harris, and pulling up the rear was Private Clegg, easily spotted with a bandage encircling his head. They had been gaining for the last two hours, and Tucker himself made no effort to hide his tracks. With Dilly, it would be futile. What Tucker had been doing was crisscrossing the country, all the while cutting Henny's sign but leading the troopers away from it. He didn't want the cavalry anywhere near Henny Cauther—they'd just trample over Henny's tracks, and Tucker would never find Justice.

Tucker mounted Barney and headed out, keeping just under the rim of the hills. He didn't need to make it easier for Dilly than it already was.

Tucker bent low over the saddle, following Henny's trail northwest in the direction of the Swede's ranch. Just like the liveryman thought he'd do. Tucker headed straight south—he had Henny's direction and could pick up his sign later. As much as he didn't want to fall too far behind him, Tucker needed to shake the army patrol. Or at least discourage them from following him any longer.

Tucker picked the spot where he could discourage the cavalry. Between two rock formations twice as high as a horse and rider sat sandstone boulders, black and brown and cracked, loosened by time, seeming to teeter over the edge of a deep canyon. Just waiting for Tucker to give them a push.

A large cottonwood log—perhaps uprooted by one of the brief but violent flash floods in this part of the territory—lay rotting off to one side of the high formation. He dismounted beside the rocks and picked his way to the top of the hill. His hand rested on one of the rocks—piled high and haphazardly, like an errant child stacking his toys—and it teetered on the edge. He threaded one end of his rope through the hondo and looped it over the boulders.

He peered around the rocks to the rolling prairie he'd come from. The soldiers had closed the distance, and, in another hour, they would catch him.

Tucker slid down the hillside and strung his rope over another large rock. He dragged the cottonwood log so that it bore weight on the rope looped over the boulders and tied it off. If things played out right for him, the log would bear its entire weight on the rocks overhead, and they'd crash down on the troopers.

If things went his way.

If his aim was true. Tucker just hoped that Dilly would be too busy studying the ground to spot the dead-man until it was too late. It was Tucker's only chance to throw them off his trail.

He rode off to the west several hundred yards and down a gully deep enough to hide Barney. Tucker tied the reins around a scrub juniper—loose, so that he could ride fast away from there afterwards—and slipped the Sharps from the scabbard.

He crawled to the rim of the gully and took off his coat. He bunched it up so he could lay the fore end of his rifle on it and loaded one .50 caliber shell. He stripped another from his cartridge belt and held it between his fingers. Just in case he missed that first shot.

Tucker blew warm air onto his hands, keeping his trigger finger limber. His hand had begun to stiffen from his fight with the soldiers—one knuckle broken, another sliced from the big sergeant's teeth—and he needed his gun hand pliable, ready. He might only get one shot. He settled in behind the gun.

He heard the snort of a horse before he actually saw Dilly ride through the rocks. He bent low over the side of the saddle studying Tucker's trail with the other soldiers close behind him. Tucker would have loved to spring the ambush just as Dilly cleared the rocks. But he needed to slow the troopers, inflict as much pain as he could by this one act. Letting the main group ride through would ensure most of the soldiers would be scrambling for safety in a moment.

He waited until Sergeant Harris had ridden through, with two more soldiers close behind. Tucker took up slack on the rear trigger to set it and let his breath out. And pressed the front trigger. The Sharps bucked hard, the recoil sending waves of pain through his wounded shoulder. But when he wiped the tears of pain from his eyes, he saw his slug had cut the rope.

The log fell, stretching the rope tight against the rocks, and brought the boulders overhead crashing down. Horses reared. One rock hit Sergeant Harris on the back and knocked him from his horse, while another drove into the lead trooper's horse.

Horses bucked soldiers off and ran riderless across the prairie. In the melee, Dilly fought to control his rearing buckskin, losing its footing, and Dilly threw himself off before the horse rolled on top of him.

All totaled, Tucker counted six horses that had ridden off, frightened by the sudden onslaught of rocks raining down upon them. It would take hours to round up their mounts, giving Tucker enough time to could find Henny Cauther and track him to Justice.

Tucker shucked the spent shell casing and pocketed it. He would reload it later, when he had the time to melt old bullets and buy some powder.

He gathered up his coat and started to where his mule waited. Right before he scooted down the bank, he looked back at the chaotic scene and thought Dilly looked his way and mouthed something.

Chapter 18

Tucker kept checking his back trail. No soldiers pursued, and he continued following Henny's tracks. The fool had made no attempt to hide his trail since leaving town, and Tucker could only surmise he was either stupid or thought no one would come after him. He thought back to what the law knew about Henny Cauther. He'd been too young to fight for the Confederacy, but his association with his older half brother still made him a target for the army. He had been credited with killing and raping at least two young girls from the same farm family outside Davenport, Iowa, along with another, even younger girl he had snatched right out of church services in Kansas. What interested the army the most was a witness to Henny killing a trooper and stealing his horse last year around Lincoln.

He'd been on the run with Justice and his gang ever since, which should have given him some idea how to evade capture. Tucker concluded Henny foolishly failed to hide his trail simply because he was scared. Frightened like a muskrat that's been cornered by a mink. He might be that frightened after seeing Elias Gates gunned down. Henny had made camp only once, remaining only long enough to build a fire and eat. Tucker found prairie chicken bones beside a campfire that hadn't been doused, hadn't been covered, and Henny had lit out after eating his meal tonight.

Would he hole up somewhere until morning? When the sun set in another half hour, the temperature would plummet thirty degrees by morning. *I hope you find someplace warm and away from the Sioux,* Tucker said to himself. The last thing he wanted was for Henny to freeze to death out here. Tucker needed the fool alive and laying tracks that would lead him to Justice.

He couldn't take the chance that Henny was savvy enough to lay up until morning, so he continued following the tracks.

When darkness dropped over the territory like the Lakota's *Wakan Tanka* had tossed a blanket over the sky, the horse with the chipped right hoof grew more difficult to follow. Tucker dismounted and held Barney's reins loosely as he bent and spotted each track Henny's horse made.

Tucker had used a small miner's lamp to track on moonless nights, but he wasn't sure just how close Henny was. With the nighttime prairie hiding her secrets so well, Tucker found it hard to estimate the age of Henny's tracks. Those he saw could have been made within the past few hours. Or they could have been made by Henny's horse mere moments ago. Tucker had no way of knowing, and the lamp would alert Henny if he were near.

Tucker had walked another mile in the darkness when Barney snorted, surprised, and the mule looked off to the south. A line of rolling hills abraded into a deep coulee loomed like a ghost in the darkness, the wind-swept ground contrasting with the surrounding snow.

He watched Barney. The mule focused his attention on that deep ravine in line where Henny's tracks led, fifty yards farther west. Tucker stood stock still, sensing what Barney sensed, until he spotted a standing soldier holding the reins of several horses down over the rim of the bank, his body just visible sticking above the bank of the gully.

Tucker cursed himself under his breath: *he* was the fool to think the soldiers would wait until all their horses had been captured before resuming their pursuit. Dilly had led the soldiers still on horseback. They had leapfrogged ahead of Tucker and had laid an ambush.

But how many soldiers? Tucker saw six horses flee when the boulders toppled down on the column of riders. He would guess two or three soldiers still on horseback would have been tasked with rounding up the frightened animals. If the rest broke off to catch Tucker, that meant there were six or seven soldiers waiting in the darkness ready to exact their revenge.

After he led Barney into a thicket of scrub junipers and tied him, Tucker eased his Sharps from the scabbard; then he put the rifle back. When the shooting started, he would have no time to fight with such an unwieldy gun as the buffalo rifle. It was too slow and heavy.

He studied the terrain. He could approach the soldiers down in the coulee if he walked another ravine paralleling it. Again, in his mind, he struggled with how many had ridden with Dilly. Tucker didn't want gunplay, but if those soldiers who pursued him were like the drunks running out of the saloon hell-bent on ventilating him, he might not have a choice.

He walked hunkered over until he reached the gully. He slid down on his butt, careful that rocks didn't roll down with him, careful his clothes didn't scrape against cactus and sage. When he reached the bottom, he paused to listen. The wind blew strong from the west, and Tucker heard the soldiers whispering among themselves. He walked parallel to the coulee hiding the troopers until he guessed they were only ten yards over in the next ravine.

He turned his belt so that his pistol was towards his back and it wouldn't scrape on the ground and let his hat dangle on his back by the chin strap. And, like a predatory snake that smelled fresh prey, he drew his Bowie and slithered out of the ravine. He low-crawled across the few feet separating him from the ravine where the soldiers hid. Their voices became louder as he neared, and Tucker saw the faint flicker of a campfire, previously hidden from view in the bottom of the washout. Tucker would never have allowed the troopers a hot camp if they pursued a dangerous enemy. Dilly wouldn't have, either. Perhaps he *wasn't* with them. Perhaps one of the boulders had fallen on him . . .

A cavalry horse whinnied, a trooper holding the reins only twenty yards away. Tucker peeked over the rim and counted six horses. His gaze was drawn to the campfire, and he looked away. When his eyes had adjusted to the darkness once more, he looked about. Four soldiers sat warming their hands around the fire. Sergeant Harris wasn't among them, but Private Clegg was. Blood had soaked through and onto his boots, his trousers were blackened with dried blood that contrasted with the snow, and he stared at the flames through a thick bandage circling his head.

Five soldiers, including the man assigned horse duty.

But six horses.

With the last soldier unaccounted for, Tucker scoured the darkness. One man lurked out here. Had they set a trap to lure Tucker into the soldiers' camp?

The scrape of a boot behind him seemed louder than it should have, but sound carries well on a cold night, and he chanced a look back over his shoulder. The sixth soldier squatted behind a sagebrush, his Springfield across his knees, blanket about his shoulders as he shivered. His concentration was on the other soldiers, and Tucker faded away from the campfire.

He worked his way behind the last trooper, who still stared at the others warming themselves, unaware that his life was about to change abruptly.

Tucker silently crept up behind the man.

Tucker's boot kicked a pebble along the ground.

The soldier's head jerked around to see . . .

Tucker lunged and clamped a hand over the trooper's mouth. He struggled, but to little effect. With the butt of his knife, Tucker struck him on the base of the neck. As he slumped in Tucker's arms, he dropped his rifle, and Tucker caught it before it fell. He eased the man and his gun onto the ground.

He crept back toward the shallow end of the coulee. The soldier holding the horses had gotten tired of his job, and he'd tied the mounts to a rock before joining the others clustered around the fire. They smoked and joked amongst themselves, oblivious that the man they sought had emerged from the darkness to stand mere feet away.

When Tucker cocked his Remington, they stopped their joking. "I've got exactly five rounds in this gun of mine," Tucker said, covering the troopers.

They looked at one another. One whispered. Another soldier nodded his head slightly.

"I don't like the look of you fellers," Tucker said. He sat on a rock where he could cover all of them. "Someone makes a plan. Someone else thinks it's a good idea. Except when those fools try to pull it off, somebody always winds up dead. Maybe five somebodies. Now what do you fellers say—you want to live until the morning?"

"You going to kill us or just talk about it?" Private Clegg said as he looked at Tucker with his one good eye, the other bandaged, where Tucker had cut him with the bottle. " 'Cause if you are, I might just go for my gun and see what happens."

He stood and hobbled away from the others.

"Sit down, or I'll smash your other knee," Tucker said.

A corporal—wild-eyed as the flames reflected off his face—grabbed the private and pulled him to the ground. "Don't be a damn fool, Clegg. You'd never get close to your gun."

"Smart man," Tucker said and motioned for the soldiers to

sit closer together. "Collect all the guns, Corporal."

The soldier, a man in his twenties but with the leathered face of someone who'd soldiered all his life, stood without comment and went to each man. He gathered their guns and stood beside the fire holding them.

"Just toss them in the brush."

"What do you intend to do with us?" The corporal asked after he'd flung the guns aside.

"Maybe the same as you intended doing to me if you had caught me."

The soldier looked at the ground. "It's just that a civilian can't go around beating an army sergeant, and knifing a private—"

"The hell I can't." Tucker felt his anger rise. "If your Captain Roush hadn't ordered this one"—he kicked Private Clegg's injured knee, and he winced in pain—"and that big bastard to beat me, I wouldn't have had to. Now grab that rope hanging off that saddle, and tie everyone up. And make sure you use one of those fancy knots the army teaches you. I'd hate for anyone to get loose and get shot accidentally."

The corporal did as Tucker ordered, running the rope to each man in turn and tying his hands securely. "Turn around," Tucker ordered when the others had been secured. He tied the corporal's hands and shoved him onto the ground beside the others.

"This ain't going to take us long to get shut of this rope," Private Clegg said. "Then we're coming after you."

Tucker laughed. "How, on foot? Your horses are going to be scattered hell to breakfast in just a moment."

Tucker holstered his gun and walked to the horses tied to the rock. He had grabbed his Bowie and bent to cut the reins when he heard the sound of a pistol cock behind him. "Make sure all you got in your hand is that big 'ol knife of yours when you turn around."

Dilly McMasters emerged from the darkness pointing a gun at Tucker's chest. Fire shone off his red hair, and his green eyes sparkling with anticipation. "Seems like last time it was you had the gun, and me left holding a knife."

"How long you been out there?" Tucker nodded to the dark fringes of the campfire.

"Long enough for you to think you were home free." Dilly laughed. "Do you really think I'd have let these soldiers build a fire you could see for a mile?"

"Cut us loose," Private Clegg said. "We got us some payback we need to hand out."

"Not just yet," Dilly said. "Me and Ol' Tuck here's got us a dance coming."

"What's the tune?" Tucker asked. "Or are you too afraid to put your gun away so we can have a fair fight?" He waved his knife hand at the troopers. "What ya' say—just two old friends in a draw-down. With all these here boys as witnesses?"

Dilly smiled. "You'd like that, wouldn't you? But I wouldn't face you in a stand-up gun fight for all the money in St. Louis. But"—he motioned to Tucker's Remington—"I do want you to skin that gun with your left hand. Real careful like, and toss it aside."

"So you can kill an unarmed man?"

"Tucker. Tucker. You *are* armed. You got a knife. Now toss that gun aside."

"Cut us loose, McMasters," the private screamed, struggling against the rope. "We got a right to take a chunk off his hide first."

"I'll let you do just that," Dilly said as Tucker tossed his pistol aside. "If there's any hide left when I finish."

Dilly kept his gun on Tucker as he took off his coat. He hung it on top of a sagebrush and moved to a clear part of the coulee in front of the fire. He slowly took off his gun belt and hung it on the sage beside his coat before holstering his gun. He smiled and drew two knives from his belt, smaller than skinning knives, yet the straight-bladed, razor-sharp steel reflected the flames. "This here's the tune, Tuck. We'll be doing what we should have gotten out of our system two years ago."

"Now who's at a disadvantage?" Tucker said. "I've had my fun with a knife now and again, but . . . well, your reputation is something else. If all you're doing is showing these soldiers how handy with those things you are—"

"That's not what I intend, but they'll see it for themselves soon enough. Thing I want right now is little pieces of your flesh hanging off the end of my blade and . . ."

Dilly lunged. He barely came up to Tucker's chest and was half again as light, but his small size was his advantage. He flicked blades faster than Tucker could follow, slicing off pieces of skin from either side of Tucker's neck.

Tucker lashed out with the Bowie, but Dilly had danced back out of reach.

"I could have just as easily buried my blades into your neck and bled you out right there, but I was . . . humane—"

Tucker lunged, but his knife carved the empty air as Dilly stepped out of the way and slashed Tucker on the cheek in passing. "You're just too slow," he laughed. "But I admire you for trying."

Tucker wiped sticky blood off his face. "I need to follow Henny Cauther's tracks," Tucker said, moving laterally, keeping out of the reach of Dilly's blades. "They murdered the saloon keeper from the Bucket of Blood and shot the hell out of Marshal Dawes's posse—"

Dilly—a blur or a shadow; Tucker wasn't sure which—stepped toward Tucker faster than he thought possible, and cut his arm in two swift movements. "Fighting's not a time for talking." Dilly grinned as he jumped back. "Or did no one ever tell you that?"

Sticky blood flowed from the double knife wounds on Tucker's arm, and he continued circling, thinking, stalling, wondering if Dilly's next lunge would be the fatal one.

"Private Clegg already cut that shoulder of yours," Dilly said as he flicked his knife.

Tucker jerked back just in time, and the knife sliced the air.

"By the looks of it, it must be giving you some grief."

"I'll live."

"Not for long," Dilly said and seemed to run past Tucker, running his blade across Tucker's leg.

Tucker's knee buckled, and he struggled to remain upright as Dilly retreated a safe distance.

Tucker staggered back. At any time, Dilly's next thrust might be the last. Tucker was powerless to do anything about it. Except . . .

He made a wide circle away from Dilly, moving closer to the fire. Closer to the hot embers. Closer to Tucker's only salvation.

Dilly feinted left, and Tucker moved to the left to counter him but saw the ruse too late. Dilly's blade pierced Tucker's jacket, just grazing his side, and he threw himself sideways. He allowed himself to fall on his back, close to the fire.

Dilly moved in for the kill but paused. "I wonder what's going through your mind, now that I am about to end this little dance—"

Tucker shot his hand into the fire and grabbed a flaming piece of juniper. As Dilly stood lecturing Tucker, he flung it hard at the small man's head. The wood struck Dilly full in the face, hot embers attacking his eyes, sticking to his cheek as he clawed his head and neck to clear himself of the burning coals.

As Dilly danced with the flaming firewood and rubbed his eyes with snow, Tucker struggled to his knees and drove his blade deep into Dilly's chest. Tucker ripped the wide-bladed knife up and stepped back to allow Dilly to fall next to the fire. Blood oozed out of his mouth as he tried forming words but could not.

The last thing he heard was Tucker telling him: "Fighting's not a time for talking." Tucker breathed deeply, bending over to catch his breath, blood dripping onto the fresh snow from a half-dozen wounds. "Or did no one ever tell you that?"

Dilly's movement stopped, and the soldiers sat with eyes wide, wondering—Tucker was sure—if they were next. He wiped his blade on Dilly's shirt before he walked to his gun and picked it up.

"You going to kill us, too?" the corporal asked.

Tucker blew dirt off the cylinder of his Remington and holstered it. "Why would I do that?"

" 'Cause we witnessed that." The soldier nodded to Dilly's lifeless body.

"You witnessed Dilly goading me into a fight. That's all you saw." He stepped to Private Clegg and kicked his bloody boot. "And if any swinging dick ever says I murdered Dilly, I'll see he never lies again."

Tucker walked to the horses and began untying the reins.

"You really are going to leave us afoot?" one of the soldiers asked. "That'd be the same as killing us, cold as it is."

Tucker thought about that: it *would* be the same. Without food and some heavy clothing—perhaps a blanket to keep them from freezing to death—it would be like killing them. And all he wanted was to ensure they couldn't follow.

He went to each mount and stripped the saddlebags off. He tossed them beside the fire and slapped the horses on their rumps. Their hoofbeats soon were lost in the noise of the biting wind. He had started to where he'd tied Barney when Private Clegg yelled after him, "You're not going to leave us here all trussed up!"

"Like you said before: it's not going to take you long to get out of them ropes."

Chapter 19

Justice had just run a cleaning rod through the bore of his rifle when the sound of hoofbeats, fast and desperate, approached. He whistled at Gall. "Get up on the roof of that shed."

Gall slung his rifle over his shoulder and climbed a ladder leaning against the Swede's shack. The shed lay miles to the east of the Swede's house, and he'd apparently used it during calving season by the look of the tack and branding irons hanging on an inside wall. It was an excellent place to fire down on someone.

Justice squatted behind the water-well head and levered a round into his Winchester.

Henny rode toward them on the trail the Swede long ago constructed to get into Hellion, wildly slapping his horse's neck with the reins, looking back as if he were being pursued by the devil himself. He skidded to a stop beside the well and dismounted. He bent over as he caught his breath, his wind coming in painful gasps.

Gall scrambled down from the barn and walked to the water well.

"Someone after you?" Justice said. He stood and moved to keep an eye on the road as he talked to his brother. "And where's Elias?"

"Dead," Henny sputtered. He held his stomach and sucked in air. "Gunned down in town."

"Dead? That can't be. Nobody could take Elias." Justice long ago figured no one would ever suspect Elias of riding the trail with the likes of the Cauthers. He had gotten them out of scrapes far worse than they'd see in the territory by being so ordinary looking. Justice grabbed Henny by his lapels and stood him erect. "What the hell happened?"

"Ashley," Henny breathed. "Ashley. Shot and killed Elias."

Justice swayed, and he grabbed onto the well. Elias Gates was his oldest living friend, as least as much of a friend as Justice could ever develop. Elias had impressed Justice from that first time he saw him in the North's Elmira prison camp, stealing from other prisoners too weak or too cowardly to resist. His ruthlessness had impressed Justice so much, he brought the Norwegian into his gang the moment he decided to form one after slipping past the Pinkertons at Boston port. "Just tell us what happened to Elias," Justice ordered.

Henny dipped the water ladle into the bucket sitting on the well and slurped. "Like I said, Ashley beat him to the draw—"

"Not like Elias to give a man an even chance," Justice said. Elias had always been more concerned with winning a fight than fair rules—something Justice admired.

"Just tell us how it went down," Gall pressed. He took the ladle from Henny and dropped it back into the bucket. "Elias wasn't slow on the draw, even if he was"—he looked at Justice—"a back-shooter."

"All right," Henny began, "it went down like this: Elias had Ashley dead to rights. I thought he was going to shoot him. Why he even talked to Ashley first is beyond me—"

"Professional courtesy," Gall said. "One killer to another." Gall slid his rifle back into his scabbard. "My guess is Gall wanted Ashley to sweat a little."

"Just tell us what the hell happened," Justice pressed.

Henny nodded. "All right—Elias *was* going to shoot Ashley. He had the drop on him, what with Ashley's gun in his holster and his hands in his pockets."

"Smart man," Gall said. "Given Ashley's reputation."

"Still don't explain how Elias got hisself killed," Justice said, impatient. He just wanted Henny to explain what happened, and he glared at Gall to shut him up. "Tell us with no more damned interruptions."

Henny sat on the cold ground holding his head. "Some army NCO stuck his gun in Elias's back. Made him holster. Said Ashley deserved a fair chance. When Elias acted like he was walking away, he drew his gun. But Ashley shot him. Twice. Just as quick as that." He snapped his fingers.

"Where were you when all this was going on?" Justice demanded.

"I seen everything from the livery. I was waiting with the horses for Elias to drill Ashley—"

"You seen all this and did nothing?" Justice's face instantly turned crimson, and heat drifted up his neck despite the cold. "You did nothing to help Elias?"

Henny nodded. "I couldn't do anything. He'd of killed me, too—"

Justice wrenched Henny from the ground and slapped him hard across his face. He fell to the ground, and Justice kicked him hard in the side. When Henny rolled in the snow, holding his gut, Justice grabbed him by the coat front. He hoisted him erect and backhanded him. He had cocked his fist to throw a punch when Gall grabbed onto Justice's arm. "Whoa, boss. Henny's just a kid—"

"Who let Elias get hisself killed." He jerked his hand away, but Gall grabbed his arm again. "Last thing you told Elias to do was to keep Henny hid 'cause his face was on the Wanted posters same's us. Seems like that's just what he done."

Justice's hand fell limp at his side, and he dropped Henny, who fell to the ground and held his face, which had become as red as embers.

Justice sat on the well head and breathed deeply. Were it not for Gall stopping him, Justice might have beaten his half-wit brother senseless. Or worse. The too-familiar rage had consumed him, much as it had during the war. Much as it had whenever his orders were ignored by the people they robbed. But Gall was right—Justice *had* wanted Elias to keep Henny safe.

Justice stooped and helped his brother stand. He sat Henny next to him on the well, but Henny cringed and tried moving away. "I'm all right now," Justice said, feeling his breathing slow, regaining his composure. He took his Bull Durham pouch and began rolling two smokes. "Just tell us what y'all did in town. Did Elias find out if the soldiers are hunting us?"

Henny warily accepted the cigarette Justice offered him. "Elias went in the saloon to see what he could find out from the soldiers. When he came out, he said they weren't hunting us. They was looking for some Lakota that had raided an Arikara camp along the Missouri. We was fixing to ride out when he spotted Ashley coming in on that mule of his. After he went into the saloon, Elias went in after him. Said he was going to find the biggest soldier and tell them Ashley thought they were stupid for not locating the Indians yet. Figured the soldiers would take care of Ashley for us."

"But Ashley must have survived whatever beating he had coming."

Henny nodded. "Elias came busting out of the saloon. 'Ashley's getting the better ov them blue bellies,' he said. 'He's whippin' their asses. I cannot let him ride out of town.' And we waited in the livery for him to come out of the saloon."

"So, Ashley's alive?"

Henny rubbed his swelling jaw and nodded.

"Probably following your tracks right here." Justice reared his fist back, and Henny wilted, putting his hand up to fend off the blow when it came. "I ought to beat you like an errant stepchild. You didn't do a damn thing to hide your trail, did you?"

"I had to ride fast," Henny blurted out. "Had to get back as fast as I could to warn you."

Justice dropped his fist. "Sometime I think I should have drowned you when you were a pup. Stupid bastard." He turned to Gall. "With this genius here leading Ashley right to us, I'm thinking you ought to drop back and give him a proper welcome."

"I'd be happy to take him out," Gall said, "unless he's heading for his posse wandering around lost somewhere in the territory." He nodded in the direction of the Swede's house, which lay several tall hills to the west. "But it might be better just to pay the Swede a visit like we planned. Take that cash he's supposed to have stashed in his house and leave the territory. Way I heard it, the old man's got enough money we could live like kings in Canada."

"Mexico's warmer," Justice said. As he aged, he yearned more and more for a temperate climate. "A whole lot warmer."

"With prettier girls," Henny said, his voice wavering, excited even as he spoke about women. "And the young *senoritas* need a strong man to show them what to do."

Justice walked to his bedroll and began rolling it tight. "Then it's settled: after we pay the Swede a visit, we'll head south to Mexico," Justice said, knowing that he'd change their plans after they visited the Swede. Justice owed Ashley from before. Owed him for making his life so miserable once. And with Tucker Ashley killing Elias like he had, he'd opened up a wound in Justice that could never close until Ashley lay dead. But Gall and Henny didn't need to know that. "We'll head south then."

"And part ways after visiting the Swede?" Gall said. "After we divvy up our share?"

Justice nodded.

"Who gets Elias's cut?" Henny asked.

Justice felt rage well within him again. For a brief moment, he thought that Henny had allowed Elias to get himself killed just to have more money for himself. But Justice knew Henny wasn't that smart. "I'll see to it his wife gets it."

"Elias didn't have a wife," Gall said.

"Then I'll see it's spent wisely south of the border," Justice said. "In memory of Elias."

Justice followed the others as they rode slowly towards the Swede's ranch house. He dragged a sagebrush by a rope behind him, lightly obliterating their tracks. Now and again, he grabbed rocks from a pouch tied to his saddle and dropped them behind them. Henny had laid an easy trail to follow up to here. But from now on, it would take Ashley twice as long to work out their tracks. That he'd be able to trail them, Justice was certain. Nothing he'd done had fooled the man so far. But confounding Ashley would give them just enough time to visit the Swede. Just enough time to find the perfect ambush site to greet Ashley from when he came.

CHAPTER 20

Barney walked patiently behind Tucker as he studied the tracks. He stood erect and arched his back, feeling older than he had in years. Dilly had opened wounds in his cheek and neck, grazing his side, cutting a shallow groove into Tucker's leg. He'd had worse injuries during the war, worse injuries still when a buffalo bull gored him on a hunting trip to the Shining Mountains his first year out west.

But his shoulder worried him: it needed attention. After he rode away from the tied-up soldiers last night, he had debated whether to find the posse and get help suturing the knife wound, or go after Henny Cauther and pick up the posse afterwards. He had to take Sgt. Donnely's word that he'd tell Jack Worman the posse was wandering somewhere around Silver Springs. He had to believe Jack would slip away from the army and locate them. If Tucker waited for them to catch up, he might never pick up Justice's trail.

Of course, if Jack located Will and his merry men, they might be farther along on Justice's trail. Tucker had used valuable time leading the cavalry away from Henny's tracks, and Jack—if Donnely got the word to him—might actually be closer to the gang. The thought made Tucker shudder: the posse had proven no match for the Cauthers so far, and there was no reason to think they might have improved their chances for survival since yesterday. Even with Jack along.

Tucker decided to press on during the night. After killing

Dilly, the army would redouble their efforts to find Tucker. It would take the soldiers hours to free themselves, many more to find even one of their horses. But if Roush decided to catch up with Dilly's bunch . . . Tucker pushed the thought from his mind. He needed clarity now more than ever. He needed to think only of finding Henny. And Justice.

After tracking Henny all night, Tucker had come upon the Cauthers' camp at first light. He approached the small calving shed and quickly searched it before he bent to the fire. The coals still emitted heat, and Tucker smelled tea: Justice Cauther had stayed at the fire long enough to have a refreshing cup of hot tea before moving on.

He walked back into the shed where the Cauthers had taken refuge last night out of the wind. Only two men had laid their blankets out—Gall and Justice. Henny hadn't arrived before they broke camp in the morning. He had ridden hard all through the night and made better time than Tucker figured he would.

But the trail grew nonexistent from them on, and Tucker knew why. He had trailed Justice Cauther this last week, reading the man every time he threw down a false trail, every time he exaggerated tracks leading to an ambush. Tucker's admiration for the man grew, and yet it was hatred for such a cruel murderer that overrode admiration. Justice had wanted his trail hidden now, wanted Tucker to burn up time working it out, knowing that he would pick up the trail in time. But time wasn't Tucker's friend. He had to find the Cauthers before they left the territory. Or before they killed anyone else.

But the trail had grown as cold as the prairie winds that blew the snow clear from the ground. Tucker had ridden a semicircle a quarter mile from the camp when he finally spotted an overturned rock. He dismounted and picked up the stone. He turned it over and scratched it with his fingernail. Shale. Like that found on the banks of rivers and creeks. Except there were no rivers or creeks here, and Tucker picked up another a few feet farther on. Shale. Justice had tossed them here to make things appear natural, and it would have fooled most man trackers. Except Dilly and Tucker. And Dilly was dead.

Tucker untied his tarp and dragged it beside him. The tarp lightly brushed the snow free from the ground until he spotted a hoof print scuffed when a horse had walked over a fallen oak branch; a chipped print that dug in when the rider put the spurs to his horse. Henny's horse.

Tucker had a direction at last. The gang was headed straight for the Swede's ranch, the last place the Cauthers would be able to find fresh water before they rode into the stark Badlands.

Tucker so wanted a strong cup of coffee, anything that would fight the chill that followed his every move. He had ridden all night, and fatigue had taken its toll. But he couldn't afford to stop long enough for that cup. And if he did, he might not get going again.

So he coaxed Barney towards the Swede's and dozed. No matter how he bundled his coat around him, or how tightly he gathered his bandana around his neck to retain scant body heat, the intense chill never left him. He repositioned the other bandana sopping up blood from his shoulder, aching mightily even though he'd stopped the bleeding. His neck throbbed from Dilly's knife cuts, and his leg had begun to stiffen along with his broken knuckles.

Still, there was no end in sight.

Chapter 21

The early afternoon sun shining at a low angle made the Cauthers' trail easier to pick up. The sun cast shadows in depressions that stood out in the snow, and Tucker coaxed Barney into a trot when . . .

. . . a blur out of his periphery caught his eye. A coyote, running flat-out. Running from what?

He grabbed his binoculars and scanned the area. He saw nothing to indicate what had spooked the animal, yet something had.

At best, the soldiers had just managed to free themselves from their ropes,and started capturing their horses. Roush might even have caught up with them by now and started on Tucker's trail. But he doubted it. Roush was not a brave man, and that night in the saloon had sobered him up, if that were possible.

Tucker rode to the tallest hill on the Swede's ranch and glassed the area from where the coyote had fled. Nothing. He knew things often looked different from different angles, and he walked Barney along the ridge line, not wanting to stay atop there any longer than necessary when . . .

. . . perhaps a mile or more to the east, a line of three horsemen rode slowly, taking their time, picking their route to leave the least bit of tracks in case the army were on their trail.

Lakota.

And they led a large Belgian mare with a white blaze.

Tucker brought the binos down and rubbed his eyes. So, they

had found John. Tucker could only hope he had died quickly. The fat man had probably passed out, just like he predicted. But even if he had seen the Sioux in time, he was in no shape to defend himself. Tucker told himself he would find John's body on the way back to Ft. Pierre and give him a proper burial, knowing that was a hollow promise. By now John's bones were scattered by the prairie critters needing a quick meal.

There would be no help from the territorial marshal, but Tucker hadn't expected it. As with most fights he had got himself roped into, he would go this one alone; he was certain.

He raised the binoculars, and watched the Lakota for the briefest time before a gully swallowed them up. *They must have some kind of hate in them,* he said to himself. They would pick their time, pick their spot, but they would attack. They would have their justice.

Tucker was just as certain Justice Cauther needed his own kind of justice administered.

He stowed the binoculars and continued toward the ranch house.

Black smoke rose over the horizon even before Tucker topped the low rise overlooking the Swede's ranch yard. What burned, he could not immediately identify, but something told Tucker it wouldn't be good news for him.

He brought the binos down and rubbed his eyes as he thought back to what Jack once told him about the Swede. Konrad Lundgren—a Dane whom everyone called the Swede because it rolled off the tongue easier—had braved Lakota war parties raiding his livestock. He had found—and lynched—two cowboys from Kansas he caught with a running iron and trailing his cattle last year. Lundgren had lost two sons in gunfights defending the homestead, and another in childbirth. He was left with one daughter whom his wife had given birth to twelve years ago. Through it all, Lundgren had prevailed, increasing the size of his herd with each passing year. And he owned the only fresh-water pond for fifty miles.

Barney balked, and his nose flared. Tucker pulled him up short and followed the mule's gaze. Black smoke boiled skyward from in back of the ranch house, and Tucker coaxed Barney down the hill while he shielded his eyes from the sun. From a quarter mile, he saw men walk from the ranch house to a spot behind the corrals. Two men slung over their shoulders what, at this distance, appeared to be rifles, while a third man stood looking down at the ground. Tucker slipped his Sharps from the scabbard and picked his way slowly down the hill towards the Swede's house.

Jack Worman worked the business end of a pick while Ronnie shoveled dirt into a hole in the ground. Marshal Dawes came out of the house with a bandana covering his nose, and Pasqual walked around the barn carrying a load of wood in his arms. Jack arched his back when he saw Tucker approach and laid the pick aside. Tucker hadn't seen Jack in months, yet they didn't shake hands. No handshake was needed.

"Jesus, you look like hell," Jack said. Tucker winced when Jack touched his cheek where Dilly had cut him. "And I see you're favoring one leg."

"I'll survive." Tucker nodded to a grave marker fashioned out of barn wood. "The Swede?"

"His daughter," Jack said.

"And it's a good thing you weren't here when we found them." Will tossed a rag doll into the hole. "It would give you nightmares what we found, like it's fixin' to give us."

"You said you found 'them'?"

Ronnie motioned to a blanket on the ground. A lady's pointed lace-up boot stuck out the end. "The Swede's wife," Ronnie said.

"Shame, too," Jack said. "She was a nice lady. She was one of them catalogue women the Swede brought here from Massachusetts before this was a territory." He looked away. "She fed me the best wild plum pie I ever had whenever I stopped by. She was a good woman."

"More markers." Pasqual walked away from them with an armload of barn planks, and his bandana covered his nose and mouth. "Wasn't enough left of the grainery to get any wood."

"The fire out back?" Tucker asked.

Pasqual jerked his thumb over his shoulder. "The Cauthers torched the grainery. They didn't want to give us the benefit of the Swede's oats and wheat. That black smoke is from the kerosene. They took the Swede's fresh horses and shot theirs. Figured we'd better burn the critters."

"I figured they didn't want us to have any horseflesh better than ours." Jack pointed to shallow graves. "Drop the planks there. We'll need them."

Tucker looked over the scene. "I hear the Swede had a couple of hired hands—"

"I figure they was the first ones shot," Will said. He stood with his hands on his hips and motioned to the barn. "They're lying in back of the corral. A damned shame."

"Where's the Swede?" Tucker asked.

"Still inside." Pasqual leaned on his shovel to steady his hand enough to roll a smoke. "But I wouldn't go in there."

"Jack?"

Jack led Tucker to the house. Tucker stopped before he entered and turned to Will. "John's dead—"

"Oh, no!" said Will. "How the hell we going to get any help now?"

"I knew it," Ronnie said, throwing his shovel down. "I knew I should have just taken that mare of John's and ridden out . . . for help."

"You can still ride Sadie if you got a mind," Tucker said.

Ronnie looked sideways at Tucker. "How's that?"

"John's mare," Tucker answered. "She's not a mile back."

Ronnie smiled. "Then what's stopping us? Let's go round 'er up."

"You go fight for her," Tucker said as he watched Ronnie's reaction when he told him. "Those Sioux have her now. All you got to do is take the horse from them."

Will stepped close to Tucker. "You saying those Indians killed John and followed us here?"

"They followed *me,*" Tucker said. "But the result is still the same—you'll need to post a guard on our horses, and the camp. They'll hit us sooner rather than later."

"Crap!" Will said. "Pasqual."

Pasqual came off his tree stump and flicked his cigarette away. "Now what . . ."

"You take first watch."

"Why me?"

"Because all you've been doing is carrying around some wood for markers while the rest of us has been burying bodies."

"Take the watch yourself."

Tucker laid his hand on the gambler's shoulder. "If those Indians attack while you're sleeping again, I'll kill you myself. Now do what Will says if you want to live." He motioned to the barn. "A smart man would get up high."

Pasqual glared at Tucker, but he turned on his heels and started for the barn.

"Was that John from the blacksmith shop those Indians killed?" Jack asked as he led Tucker into the ranch house.

"The same." Tucker jerked his thumb over his shoulder. "And except for some poor bastard cowboy who got shot a couple days ago, John was the only one with sand."

"They said Gall Manahan shot some old cowboy riding with the posse."

"He did," Tucker said. "Hell, these peckerwoods couldn't fight their way out of a gunny sack, let alone go after the Cauthers."

"Or Indians," Jack added.

At first glance upon entering the house, things appeared normal: a pie safe in the kitchen—replete with legs sitting in cans filled with kerosene to keep rodents and insects out—stood open, revealing two pies awaiting supper. A rug lay just inside the door waiting for a beating from a rug broom tilted in one corner. Three sets of dirty dishes remained on the kitchen table. "Figure the Cauthers ate their fill before . . ." Jack trailed off as he motioned Tucker into the next room.

Even before they passed the doorway into the sitting room, the odor assailed Tucker's nostrils, and he caught himself retching.

"I damn near got sick myself," Jack said.

A few steps farther into the room Tucker spotted the source: next to a pot-bellied stove still putting out heat lay a corpse, his blue eyes frozen, lifeless, looking up at the paisley-papered ceiling. The man had been stripped to the waist, and parts of his flesh had been sliced off in neat, almost surgical rows. Tucker had once seen a Kiowa victim left like that, but never the victim of a white man. "I figure the Swede wouldn't tell them the combination to his safe. The old boy was just stubborn enough he wasn't going to let them steal his money."

Tucker took a blanket from a chair back and covered the corpse. "He must have finally told them." Tucker pointed to a safe in the far corner of the room. The Cauthers would have needed dynamite to blow it open, as they'd used it the last few years when it became available. But the safe remained unscathed, with the door wide open.

"He didn't tell them because they tortured *him,*" Jack said. "He told them because of his twelve-year-old daughter. We found her naked body a few feet from him," he pointed to a blood spot on the floor. "Raped."

Tucker closed his eyes, imagining the anguish the father must have felt watching his little girl being raped. Beaten, too, as her lifeless body would attest to.

"Way I figure it, only when the girl was about to be raped did the Swede tell them the safe combination. But it did no good. Looks like one—or all of the gang—had their way with her. Many times. They left the leather thong they strangled her with wrapped around her neck."

"Just like Velma," Tucker said.

Jack's jaw muscles tensed. "Marshal Dawes told me how Velma died. He said the same thing—probably the same man killed this little girl what killed my Velma."

Will waved at Tucker through the door, and he turned to Jack. "They're done digging the Swede's grave," Tucker said, mainly to get Jack's mind off his woman. "Grab his legs?"

Jack had grabbed onto the dead man's feet and Tucker, his shoulders, when Tucker dropped his end, and the Swede's head smacked the floor.

"What the hell's wrong?" Jack said as he set the body down.

Tucker explained about the fight Captain Roush had arranged, and how the little private had been handy with a blade. "Dilly's cuts were just minor ones. But that damned private cut my shoulder to the bone."

"Then sit here," Jack said. "Pasqual and Ronnie can carry the Swede out. I'll come back in a moment with my stitch kit."

"Looks like they lit out soon's they had the money," Jack said as he ladled another scoop of beans on a plate before passing it to

Ronnie. "Looks like they're making a run for Wyoming."

Tucker sat on a chair at the Swede's dining room table between Ronnie and Jack. It seemed wrong to be in the house eating the dead family's food. But he had eaten no better than the posse had the last week, and he welcomed a good meal.

Will came into the room hitching his trousers up. "Damn two-holer is cold."

"What did you expect, Marshal," Jack said. "A nice privy like you had in Sioux City?"

Will ignored Jack and sat in a chair opposite Tucker. "You got a plan to catch these animals?"

Tucker nodded. "Me and Jack's been talking." He used a checkered napkin to indicate the outline of the territory, and salt and pepper shakers to show boundaries. "Jack said the army patrols have been searching for Indians down towards the Wyoming border. That'll slow the gang down some, as they won't know if the soldiers are looking for them after murdering the Swede and his family."

"They won't be," Jack said. "Even after this, Captain Roush will not lift a finger to help civilians unless there's something in it for him." Jack laid his fork on the table. "And this is where I cut the sign of two different Sioux raiding parties." He indicated south. "That's bound to slow the Cauthers down, too, if they realize the Indians are close. Make them watch their back trail a little closer if they think they might stumble across Sioux. That's the only chance we have."

"I don't follow you," Will said.

"Here." Tucker laid a line of salt on the table. "This is the Badlands. If one group works south, towards Wyoming, and the others hug the rim of the Badlands, we might come across them."

"You mean split our forces?" Will asked.

Tucker leaned toward Will, and he scooted his chair back. "If you haven't noticed, Marshal, you don't *have* any forces. You've lost your best man in Frank North, and John's out on the prairie somewhere with arrows sticking out of his back."

Tucker stood and grabbed the coffeepot warming on the stove. "This is our only chance. Especially with the Cauthers mounted on fresh horses."

"If they hadn't burned the grain up, our horses might have been able to freshen up," Will said.

"I could have gone for help," Ronnie said. "If the Cauthers hadn't taken the Swede's horses, I could have ridden for a telegraph office."

"But you can't," Tucker said. "So no sense arguing over it. What do you say, Will—we split up and hope to run into them?"

Will studied the impromptu map. "Okay. Okay. What do you suggest?"

"Each group will need a tracker," Tucker explained. "You and me skirt the Badlands—your Appaloosa's got some spunk left, and my mule can live off anything. The rest of the horses are pretty much tuckered out, while Justice has the Swede's fresh ones. Besides, we'll need the best mounts among us if we're going into the Badlands.

"Jack and Pasqual and Ronnie will work north," Tucker said, knowing there was less chance they'd run into the Cauthers going that route. Justice Cauther—if he was anything like Tucker—would chose the route that would be harder for a posse to follow. Especially one with worn-out mounts, and worn-out men faring just as badly. Tucker and Will had the best chance of finding the gang.

"All right," Will said. "We head out at first light."

"No," Tucker said, shaking sand out of his boots before putting them back on. "We start now."

"At night?" Will said.

Trucker nodded. "That's the last thing they'll be expecting.

And the last thing the Indians will figure we'd do, too." *And just one night inside a warm house out of the elements, and the posse would never be goaded into continuing the search.*

CHAPTER 22

Justice sat on a rock outcropping, his rifle across his lap, and his head on a swivel. It had been daybreak when they'd spotted the army patrol, and it had been hours since Justice sent Gall to see where the patrol was headed. If they decided to help a civilian posse look for the gang, Justice needed to know. Elias told Henny in town that the army wasn't looking for them. But Justice knew that his piss-ant half brother was probably too scared to remember much about the night Ashley killed Elias.

"Why do we care about an army patrol?" Gall said when Justice ordered him to shadow them. "All we have to do is make a run for Wyoming, and we'll be home free. You know by now their horses gotta be played out."

"But Tucker Ashley is still on this side of the grass."

"Forget Ashley—"

"Never!" Justice had grabbed Gall by the coat front and lifted him off the ground. "I'll forget him when he's worm food."

"What *is* it with you and that Ashley feller?" Henny joined in.

Justice carefully set Gall on the ground and straightened his lapels. "Just see to that patrol."

Justice refilled his teacup and looked at the bright noonday sun. It was deceptive, like Justice himself had been, riding the killer's trail. There should have been warmth; the snow should have been melting. Yet there was no warmth as he waited for Gall.

Justice turned his back to the wind and rolled a cigarette. He lit it and watched the smoke rise high. A front threatened to dump more snow onto the ground, and the temperature had dropped twenty degrees in two hours. He had lived through wicked, unexpected storms as a mariner. She was a fussy witch, Mother Nature was, who often took her frustrations out on the wee folk. Often with fatal consequences. He had weathered the storms that came up in deadly squalls now and again. He wasn't sure he could weather this damnable frigid weather.

He took out his Waltham and carefully wound the watch; Gall had been gone four hours, and Justice began to worry that the army had killed him.

Justice extended his spyglass, looking for Gall, for the army patrol, but he saw nothing. Just the occasional fox hunting a rabbit, a hawk swooping in for the same victim. Nothing.

He snapped the glass closed as Henny scrambled up the hill. He carried a cup of tea and handed it to Justice like a peace offering.

"That ain't gonna get you in any good standing with me."

"You still mad at me, Justice?" Henny said, careful to remain just out of slapping range.

"You dumb-ass kid—why the hell did you kill that little girl?"

"I told you it would get the Swede to talk."

"I could have gotten him to talk without you dragging her from that root cellar—"

"You could only skin so much of him to know he wasn't gonna give the combination up."

"But you still didn't have to kill her."

"She was a witness." Henny stood and looked over the prairie. "Been daybreak since Gall rode out. Maybe the Indians got him. Or that army patrol. Maybe he ain't coming back." Henny grinned. "We ought to just figure that Gall's been shot, or run off and not coming back. Be more money for us. We could light out for Mexico right now—"

"You've always been a damned fool," Justice said. "Gall will return. I saw to that when I refused to split up the Swede's money right off and hung onto the take from that saloonkeeper. Gall will be back, if for nothing else than to claim his share." Justice shuddered. "Besides, the last man I'd want pissed at me is Gall Manahan with that rifle of his."

Gall rode back into camp at a fast trot. It might have been the first time Justice ever saw the man in a hurry. He jumped down from the Swede's chestnut and for once didn't head right for the coffeepot.

"Took you long enough—"

"No time to chew my ass." Gall jerked his thumb in the direction he'd come from. "Three of the posse are coming on strong. Not two miles back."

"You didn't hide your trail?"

"No time to," Gall sputtered, out of breath. "I laid up watching that army patrol pass me. When it was long past, I figured I was clear, when I caught wind of the posse. I didn't know if they seen me or not, but I knew I had to light out of there."

Justice's lip quivered with anticipation. "Ashley's mine. I'll make him suffer for killing Elias—"

"Ashley ain't with 'em," Gall said. "Some young feller I ain't never seen before is tracking for 'em. And he's good."

Justice kicked snow over the fire. "Then let's reward them for coming this far just for us."

Justice folded his spy glass and slipped it inside his vest. The three-man posse had skirted a tall butte and passed between two smaller ones. It was obvious at half a mile away that the lead man was a tracker; knew where he was going by the manner in which he bent over his paint's withers studying the ground. He'd be the dangerous one, but the one who might know the most about where Ashley was. "Keep that one alive," he told Gall. "I'd prefer at least one other man to be able to talk, but for sure don't kill that one."

Gall disappeared down a coulee just shallow enough to hide him on his way to the high hill he'd picked out. "You heard what I told Gall," Justice said. "I want that one alive."

Henny grinned. "Then I'll get one of the other ones. I bet I drop one before Gall can."

"Just get to those rocks and wait until they're within range."

Justice low-crawled to a dead-fall tree and rested his Winchester on it as he watched the three men through his ship's glass. The lead man rode slowly, deliberately, having picked up Gall's trail as he rode back after spotting the army patrol. Justice and Gall had discussed the point of no return for the posse—that point when they'd pass a mound of rocks—to begin their ambush.

The three men approached the rocks, and Justice tensed when the tracker paused. He turned in his saddle and spoke to the others. He turned back and stood in his stirrups. Something concerned him, and he scanned the prairie in front of him for long moments before continuing on.

When the lead man passed the rocks, Gall fired his rifle. The last man in the line slumped over his saddle. He seemed to dangle there like some bizarre puppet, his coat hung up on the saddle horn for a brief moment before it ripped, sending the man's lifeless body to the ground. His buckskin walked a few paces away and began munching some bluestem grass growing on a hillside.

The remaining two posse men dove from their horses as Henny and Justice began firing steadily. The tracker—trail savvy and alert—spoke to the man beside him, and they hugged the ground. They scurried to a shallow depression that barely hid them and peeked over the rim. The tracker clambered to one knee. He had shouldered his rifle and begun firing when Henny shot him. The man dropped and rolled in pain. When the second man dove for the safety of some sage brush, Justice shot him, and he fell back into the gully. He rolled over onto his back clutching his gut.

Their firing stopped, and they lay immobile in the depression filled with rabbit brush and locoweed.

"Go down there and see if they're dead."

"Me?" Henny said. "Why me?"

"Because you shot the tracker when I said not to."

"But what if they're alive? What if they kill me when I walk up on them?"

"Then it might be a blessing for me."

Henny stood slowly but made no effort to walk to the downed men.

"Go on," Justice said. "Get your sorry ass down there, or I'll shoot you my ownself."

Henny pointed his rifle in front of him like a divining rod and picked his way past rocks and sage to where the men lay.

Justice grabbed his spyglass and watched Henny approach. The tracker's head moved. His hand was covered in blood as he felt the crease on the side of his head. He was alive after all, and Justice silently thanked Henny for being such a shitty shot.

The other man might not be so lucky. Justice had meant to shoot him lower, not in any vitals, but the shot had gone high, and blood soaked the man's vest.

Justice stood and started towards the men at a fast walk. He needed to get there before the men stood and surprised Henny. *Damn kid was like a fear-biting dog that nipped at your heels. He might just shoot them out of a cowardly reaction.* And Justice needed them alive.

Chapter 23

Gall finished wrapping Jack's head with a piece of the dress that Henny had ripped from the Swede's daughter as a souvenir. Justice turned from the campfire and handed Jack a cup of stout coffee. Justice sat on a log and studied his prisoner.

"As you can see," he said, nodding to Jack's bandage, "I'm not as bad as folks claim I am."

"You certainly are a prince of a fellow; I'll admit that." Jack sipped the coffee—hot and fresh. "Almost makes me forget what you did to Velma and that little girl at the Swede's place."

"I did nothing." Justice chin-pointed to Henny, who sat on his own log and rubbed what was left of the little girl's dress between his fingers. He passed it between his hands and smelled the cloth. "Unfortunately, my half brother is also a half-wit."

Gall laughed as he poured his own cup. "Hell, Henny's not even a quarter-wit, the dumb shit he pulls."

"Point is," Justice said, glaring at Gall, "Henny gets a mite . . . carried away when it comes to the ladies."

"Just your normal character flaw, is that it?"

Justice shrugged. "I blame it on myself for not being forceful enough when he was younger. But enough of us: what about the rest of the posse?"

"Cowboy we called Ronnie's dead back where you ambushed us." Jack nodded to the third man, the one Gall had wounded. He lay on his side, moaning, rocking back and forth. But Justice was no idiot like his brother. "Pasqual and me's the only ones left."

"Young man—do you take me for a fool? Where's Tucker Ashley and the others?"

Jack forced a smile. "By now they're probably warming themselves by the fire in that saloon you robbed."

"And you can be back there, too," Justice said, "if you tell me where he is."

"Do you take me for a fool? You have no intention of letting either me or Pasqual live through this."

"Where's Ashley?" Justice shouted.

"He went to get help from the army," Jack said. "They're probably headed back here right now."

Justice pulled his Colt and tapped Jack's head with the barrel. Jack jerked back and rubbed the bandage.

"Damned liar. He'd know the army won't lift a finger to help civilians. Now if you don't tell me where the hell he is, that cup of coffee will be your last."

Jack forced a smile. "Then I got to admit that my last cup of coffee was one of the best I've ever had."

"Ashley?"

"Can't help you."

Justice pointed his pistol at Jack's head. He continued sipping his coffee, with no change to his expression.

Justice turned his gun on the gambler moaning on the ground. He rolled back and forth, holding his stomach, and Justice shoved his gun under his chin. "Maybe if he's gone—"

"Do what you got to," Jack sipped coffee. "I got no loyalties to the gambler. Lord knows he's got no loyalties to anyone else. Besides, it looks like Pasqual's not long for this side of the grass anyway."

"Then you leave me no choice," Justice said and cocked his gun.

"No!" Pasqual said.

Justice paused. "So, you are not as bad off as you let on. You might want to live, no?"

"Who doesn't?"

Justice turned his gun on Jack again. "Then you probably wouldn't tell me where Ashley is if I threatened Jack?"

A slight smiled crossed Pasqual's face. "Not on your life."

"But you would your own?" Justice jammed his gun barrel into Pasqual's stomach. "Being a gambler, you should be able to read me: I am not bluffing. This time you die. I'm tired of pissing with you. Now where's Ashley?"

"Don't say anything!" Jack shouted. He rose from the ground and lunged at Pasqual. Gall leaned over and clubbed Jack on the back of the head with the butt of his pistol. Jack fell to the snow groaning, rubbing his head, forcing himself to turn over and face Pasqual. "Don't say a thing."

"Easy for you to say," Pasqual said, keeping an eye on Justice's gun still pointed at his stomach. "You're not the one going to get himself killed in a moment." Pasqual grimaced, yet his pain didn't appear as intense as when he tried fooling Justice earlier. "Just so you know, Ashley won't stop until he finds you."

Justice sat close to Pasqual and poured himself a cup of tea. "Except for taking a job with this lousy posse, just what *does* Ashley have against me? I've never even met him."

"Velma," Pasqual answered. "The whore from the Bucket of Blood you kidnapped and killed. She was his best friend's woman"—he nodded to Jack—"his woman."

Justice saw an opening he had not hoped for before. "So, you're saying Jack and Tucker Ashley are best friends?"

Pasqual nodded.

"Can you ride?"

"I can, but not far and not fast."

"Think you can find Ashley?" Justice asked.

"No," Pasqual answered. "But he would find me if I wandered around and made enough noise. Why?"

"I want you to find him and come back. You do that, and I'll let Jackie-boy here go."

"You've got to do better than that."

Justice's eyes narrowed. "I'm listening."

"You have three hundred dollars you stole from the poker table the morning you and your bunch robbed the Bucket. I want it back."

"Let's just kill him," Gall said.

"Yeah," Henny added. He drew his gun and waved it at Pasqual. "He's in no position to bargain."

Justice mulled that over. If he let the gambler leave, he might just keep on going without getting word to Ashley. But if he actually thought he would recover his money, Pasqual would come back. Like most greedy bastards.

Justice stood and walked to his saddlebags. He grabbed a Double Eagle from his stash bag and flipped it to Pasqual. He caught the twenty-dollar gold piece and held it to the light.

"It's real," Justice said. "You come back here, and I'll give you the rest of your money."

Gall stepped between Justice and Pasqual. "Why waste the time on Ashley? We could be outta' here. Sunning ourselves on some Mexican beach by next week."

"Because he's a thorn in my side. Without him, the posse would have gotten lost and scattered after that first ambush. And Elias would still be alive."

"Bullshit," Gall said. "There's more going on between you two—more than just avenging Elias. Hell, he was just another damned Norweg—"

Justice lashed out, and his blow caught Gall in the throat. It wasn't a hard blow, or a particularly menacing one. But it had the intended effect: it shut Gall up as he lay writhing on the ground holding his throat. "I don't want to hear one bad word about Elias. He was as much a brother as"—he stepped toward Henny—"this fool."

Henny cringed and stepped back. He tripped over a rock and fell to the ground beside Gall.

Justice kicked at Henny, but he rolled away, and Justice faced Pasqual. "Just find Ashley."

Pasqual pocketed the money and stood painfully from the ground. "What do I tell him?"

"Tell him that if he wants to see his bestest friend alive, to come meet me. Alone."

"Where?"

"There's a place called Flat Top Butte up from Last Dog Creek."

"Never heard of it."

"I don't care if you haven't," Justice said. "What's important is that Ashley has."

"I'm telling you, he won't believe me. He hates me as it is."

"Sure, he'll believe you." Justice took his belt knife from the sheath and motioned to Gall. "Hold Jackie-boy here down, and set on his arm. I'm going to send something along with the gambler that'll convince Ashley his friend here is in dire straits."

Chapter 24

"It's Pasqual," Will said, pointing to a rider slowly approaching, hunched over the saddle, with blood staining his coat front.

Will and Tucker turned in the saddle and watched Pasqual ride toward them. Will stepped down from his horse and waited until he could grab onto him. Tucker grabbed Will's reins and dismounted Barney, while Will eased Pasqual onto the ground. Blood caked the front of his calfskin coat, and Tucker opened it. He pulled the shirt up and examined the wound. "Could have been worse," Tucker said as he felt Pasqual's back. "The bullet went through and through. You were lucky."

"You sure bandy that around," Pasqual said. "I damn sure don't feel lucky." Pasqual took Will's canteen and sipped lightly.

"Where's Ronnie and Jack?" Will said, scanning the way Pasqual had ridden as if expecting them to ride up behind him.

"Ronnie's dead," Pasqual said. "Jack got a nasty grazing wound to his head. Justice had me, but he let me go."

"How'd you escape?" Tucker stuffed Pasqual's bandana in the bullet hole in his side. "I imagine Justice Cauther never lets anyone go, unless they had an ace in the hole. That it?"

Pasqual sipped a last time before handing Will his canteen. "Justice has Jack all trussed up." He motioned to Will. "You got a smoke?"

Will rolled Pasqual a cigarette and lit it. Pasqual blew smoke rings heavenward as he weighed his answer. "When neither Jack nor I would tell him where you were," he told Tucker, "Justice threatened to kill Jack. I couldn't let that happen, so I volunteered to find you and bring you back." Pasqual flicked his stub away, and it fizzled in the snow. "He wants you, Tucker. Real bad. Guess killing that farmer stuck in his craw. Bad."

"How do we know you're not lying?" Will said. "I can't see Justice Cauther taking a chance and letting you go. How can we be sure you just didn't light out, leaving Jack there to fight the Cauthers by his lonesome?"

"Help me up," Pasqual said, and Will helped him stand.

Pasqual stumbled to his horse and reached inside his saddlebags. He handed Will a bandana caked with frozen blood. "Unwrap it."

Will peeled the cloth back until a finger appeared. Will dropped it on the ground, and Tucker bent to it. It was the first joint of a man's finger, sliced as cleanly as if a surgeon had cut it off. "Justice said he'd slice another of Jack's fingers off if you don't come by tomorrow. Alone."

"Then we better ride out to meet him," Will said.

"He said alone," Tucker said. "I can't risk—"

"This once, maybe you ought to think this out." Will continued staring at Jack's finger. "There's three of the gang left. A man alone would have little chance. Besides, Justice would expect us to ride back with you."

"And how do you feel about it?" Tucker asked Pasqual. "You want to ride back there knowing I'm the one Justice wants?"

"All I know is that we've come this far. Even though I'd have turned back a couple days ago, right now I just want to see this thing through. For Frank. And Ronnie."

"And it has nothing to do with him still having your poker winnings?"

Pasqual shrugged. "That, too."

"When is Justice expecting me?" Tucker asked.

"Sometime in the morning. Place called Flat Top Butte. Said

you'd know about it."

"Good," Tucker said. "We'll ride out early tomorrow morning. With the sun at our backs, Gall Manahan will be shooting into the sun. Might just give us a break. Now tell me what else you can recall about the gang."

Pasqual said when he feigned being hurt worse than he was, he heard Justice and Gall talking. "That inbred Henny Cauther said little and kept sniffing a patch of the little girl's dress. The gang all rode fresh horses stolen from the Swede's corrals and trailed one pack mare loaded down with food."

"What kind of firepower did you see?"

"Gall had some rifle big as he is with some nasty looking telescopic sight that's as long as the barrel. He kept rolling bullets in some paper he kept in the patchbox in the rifle's butt."

"And Justice?"

"Him and Henny carry.44-40 Winchesters."

Tucker nodded. Though the .44-40s had little range, they would be devastating in a fast and furious shootout at close range. But Tucker had no intention of getting close.

Chapter 25

They rode another nine miles before they pulled up to make camp for the night. Flat Top Butte would be an easy two-mile ride in the morning, and Tucker intended on being saddled and approaching the butte just as the sun peeked over the horizon.

While Pasqual gathered sage for kindling and scrub oak branches for the fire, Will had gone off to hunt something for supper. He had probably been successful—shooting what, Tucker didn't know—and his shots had echoed off the jagged rocks minutes ago. Soon, they would have something to hang over the fire.

"Ever been to that Flat Top Butte?" Pasqual asked. He dropped his armload of wood by a circle of rocks Tucker had arranged out of the wind. " 'Cause those Cauthers didn't look like they were any worse for wear after we chased them this last week."

Tucker touched a match to the sage, and it flared up. "A man can see for miles from up on the butte. Perfect spot for a sharpshooter like Gall Manahan. If he has his hideout there." The one thing Tucker had learned about the former Confederate sharpshooter was that he was unpredictable. Even though the butte's summit would be the perfect spot to shoot from, he might choose another spot.

Pasqual threw up his hands. "Great. If that plan of yours works out, we'll be sitting ducks."

"I don't see any other way," Tucker said. He went over in his mind his plan to save Jack. Pasqual was right—he and Will would be out in the open, sitting ducks for a marksman like Gall. But Tucker was counting on the sun, counting on Gall throwing that first shot from the glare, or revealing a glint from a rifle barrel or telescopic sight so that Tucker could spot him and knock him off the butte. At least that was the plan.

Will hadn't been too anxious to go through with it, either. Especially since he would be the one Gall shot at first.

"Supper at last," Pasqual said.

Will rode toward the camp with a wide grin, and an even wider badger. He tossed it beside the fire and stepped down. "Guess you'll have to dress that," he told Tucker. "Can't say I ever ate a badger."

"Can't say I ever did voluntarily," Tucker said. "Couldn't you find anything else out here that might be tougher than this?"

Will's grin faded. "Some appreciation. Next time, you go rustle us up some supper."

"Next time I'll stick with jerky," Tucker said and grabbed his Bowie.

"You take first watch," Tucker told Pasqual. "Things didn't turn out so well the last time you took the cocktail watch."

"Don't you think those Sioux have given up on us?" Will asked. He lay warming under his blankets atop his ground cloth, only his eyes, nose, and mouth sticking out. "If we're having this hard a time keeping warm, just think what it's like for them."

"You never been around Indians much, have you?"

Will shrugged. "Sure, I have. I've arrested a few for getting liquored up and fighting. And I sent one down to that new federal prison in Wyoming for breaking into that rancher's hen house last year."

"Those Indians," Tucker said, "ain't these Indians. These Lakota grow up with fighting on their mind. They live and breathe and scheme how best to steal a white man's property. And his life. They ignore things such as blizzards so cold, pump handles break, and heat so intense it would scald your skin. They have been conditioned to keep going, no matter what. You cut one bad—or shatter an arm or a leg with a lucky shot—they'll tough it out and still come after you. No, they're out there. It's just a matter of time before they make their move."

Pasqual bundled a blanket around himself and sat by the fire holding one of his hide-out guns. If one of the Indians chose to attack from right across the campfire, Pasqual had him. Other than that, Pasqual would be dead before he cocked the hammer. The only thing Tucker hoped for was that Pasqual would give enough of a warning if they attacked that Will and he could get into the fight before the Indians slit their throats.

And Tucker was convinced that tonight would be the night the Sioux attacked. They had been following him for two days. What he told Will and Pasqual was true—warriors grew up ignoring the intense cold. Like tonight. But they were human as well, and would be anxious to end their stalk with three fresh scalps and fresh horses.

Tucker would have liked to sleep close to the fire. But, more importantly, he would like to live until morning. He unrolled his blanket and tarp behind a downed box elder tree lightning had hit at one time. The bare branches were blackened, the trunk split, but it provided cover for when the Lakota sneaked into camp.

He looked over the camp a final time. Will snored loud enough to scare howling coyotes away, while Pasqual huddled under his blanket beside the fire. He had added too many branches to it—it blazed high and hot enough that the Sioux would spot it for a mile. That's what Tucker hoped. He was tired of wondering when they would attack. Tonight, he knew, the wait would be over.

Tucker slept a fitful sleep. Everything woke him with a start—the sound of an owl on a nightly hunt; the piercing scream of a cougar in some nearby canyon. And every time he woke, he peeked through the maze of burnt branches at Pasqual still shivering by the fire, and Will still snoring as if he had no care in the world. But Tucker's hand still rested on his Remington under his blanket. Right beside his extra ammunition.

Tucker had closed his eyes and dozed, when silence awakened him. Utter silence from the prairie night. Where there should have been at least a prairie lawyer howling, Tucker heard no coyotes. But he should have.

Unless something spooked them and they fled.

He fidgeted under his tarp. He needed to see a man about a horse. But he argued with himself that if he left the warmth of the blanket to visit the bushes, he never would get warm again. But he had to move, or he would pee his blanket.

He pulled the corner of the blanket back when . . .

. . . a stone rolled across the snow and hit another at the edge of the fire. Nearly soundless, he wouldn't have heard it if he weren't awake.

He bent low behind the tree and eyed the camp. Pasqual's head bobbed on his chest. His pistol had slipped from his grasp and lay in his lap.

Will had turned over once since the last time Tucker looked, and his nose was all that jutted into the frigid night air.

Tucker drew his pistol and waited and watched. The Indians were concealed somewhere in the darkness, away from the periphery of the firelight. But where?

A sage branch snapped to his left, and he saw movement in front of him, shadows working their way silently toward camp, well away from the horses. The Lakota had little interest in the white man's horses just now. That would come later. After they had killed every man in camp.

Wake up, damned fools, Tucker said to himself, but he dared not yell a warning. For doing so would let the Indians know just where he was hidden. And Tucker was their only hope right now.

The Indians stopped abruptly. Had they spotted Tucker? He slowly moved his head side to side, looking at the night in his peripheral vision, knowing images stood out clearer with a man's side vision. Two warriors squatted thirty feet from Will's feet, each holding a knife that reflected the slightest from the fire. The warriors pointed to Will and Pasqual and looked around the camp. Had they thought one of the logs blending into the snow or the blanket lying beside a saddle was Tucker?

A third Indian held a rifle at the ready as he stood ten yards behind Pasqual.

So, that was their plan—two Indians would creep into camp and silently take each of the *wasicu.* But if they should awaken and start shooting, the Indian with the rifle would use it. It was a good strategy, Tucker thought.

The two Lakota hunkered over as they approached Will and Pasqual. The man with the rifle raised it.

The *click* of a rifle hammer pulling back was loud in the cold night air.

The two Indians crouched within striking distance of Will and Pasqual.

Tucker took a breath, and exhaled, calming himself when . . .

. . . the Indians with the knives ran the last few feet, each focusing on his target, blades poised overhead.

Pasqual woke with a start and yelled.

Will struggled, screaming, to get out of his blanket and tarp.

As Will's Indian came down in a fatal arc with his knife,

Tucker fired. It caught the man on his arm, and he dropped the knife.

Pasqual kicked his legs out and stood, pivoting to meet his Indian's attack.

The Sioux fired his rifle, the bullet whizzing past Pasqual. As the Indian levered another round into the chamber, Tucker fired two quick shots, hitting the man in the chest and gut. The Indian dropped his rifle and fell beside the fire as Tucker turned his attention to the other two.

But, they were gone. Just gone. Back into the night, with the only thing to show for their effort a dead comrade.

Tucker kept behind the tree as he shucked the spent shells from his pistol and thumbed fresh ones in. "Everybody all right?" Tucker called out.

Will managed to free himself from the blanket, and he stood in bare feet waving his Colt at the air. "I'm okay, but where the hell'd they go?"

"Well, I'm not okay." Pasqual scooted closer to the fire and stripped his coat off. Blood soaked his shirtsleeve, and he held his arm across his body.

"Stay alert," Tucker told Will and dropped onto the ground beside Pasqual. "Let's see it."

Pasqual turned so that Tucker could examine the wound. "Son of a bitch damned near cut my arm off."

"It's not that bad," Tucker said. The knife had severed the arm muscle but had missed the artery. Pasqual was lucky, even if he didn't think so.

Tucker walked to his saddlebags and grabbed his stitch kit. He threaded a needle with cat gut and returned to the fire.

"Think they're still out there?" Will said.

Tucker stuck the needle in the fire for a moment before turning to Pasqual. "I told you once that the next person I sew up might be you."

"Don't be so smug," Pasqual said. He stuck a branch between his teeth. "Just get it over with."

Tucker blotted blood away and began stitching Pasqual's open wound together, while Will bent to the Lakota. He turned the warrior over. He had died instantly, bled out little, and forever looked up at the stars. Will turned away from him and brought the brave's rifle to the fire. "Spencer," he said as he opened the loading gate in the butt stock. Seven rounds spilled onto the ground from the tube magazine. "Where you suppose he got that?"

Tucker tied off the stitches and helped Pasqual lay back onto his blanket. "Best I can do for you."

He picked up the rifle and held it to the light. "My guess is he stole the rifle from the same place he got his fancy war cloth," Tucker said, motioning to the red cloth with bright yellow flowers tied to the warrior's upper arm. "John."

Will holstered his Colt and grabbed his rifle. "Think they'll be back?"

Tucker nodded. "They will, but not tonight, I figure." He put more wood on the fire, and it flared up. "Those two bucks with the fancy blades were young. That raid of the Arikara village may be their first taste of killing. If I were a betting man—like our friend Pasqual there—I'd say they'll be back. But they got to patch up the one I shot first. It wasn't a good hit, but it'll keep them busy. That'll take time."

"What do we do now?" Pasqual asked. He had turned as ashen white as the snow as he held his bandaged arm. "We're not exactly up to fighting speed ourselves."

"Only thing *to do* is stick to our plan in the morning," Tucker answered. "We still have to help Jack."

Chapter 26

Tucker bent low over Will's Appaloosa and looked over what was left of the posse. When Tucker suggested that Will wear Tucker's coat and hat and ride the mule, Will had balked. "You want me to be a decoy."

"You have a quick grasp of things," Tucker answered, swapping his Stetson for Will's Montana Peak. "Take good care of my hat—it cost me a week's pay."

"It won't fool Justice or that sharpshooter of his," Pasqual said. "I seen 'em. They're mean and tougher than boiled whale shit. You saw what they did to Jack's finger—"

"*I'll* be the sitting duck," Will pled. "*I'll* have holes drilled in me—"

"I don't think so," Tucker said. "Justice wants me, but he wants me alive. He wouldn't go to all the effort to stick around the territory—holding Jack as hostage—just to kill me outright. No, he wants me to suffer. At a distance, they won't know the difference between you and me—we're about the same size and build. My best guess is he might shoot to wound you."

"That's a hell of a relief," Will said.

"Sorry, but that's the cards you drew."

And all Will had to do was be a decoy long enough for Tucker to find Gall and take him out. "I'll stake your life on it."

"And I'm supposed to ride out in the open with *him*?" Pasqual asked. He had tied his arm tight to his chest with John's bloomers he took off the dead Indian. "I can't ride so good, what with being trussed up like this."

"You couldn't ride very well to begin with," Tucker said. He settled onto Will's horse. The Appaloosa stretched its head back as if surprised it had a strange rider. "Look: Justice is predictable. That's how we managed to stay on his trail as long as we did. Gall Manahan will start the festivities, just like he did that first ambush. If you ride close to Will, they won't want to risk shooting you for fear of hitting me. That might hold him off just long enough for me to locate him. Or throw his shot off just enough that I can spot him."

"How about if you're wrong," Will asked, "and he kills me right off?"

"Then you'll die with my promise that I'll follow Justice and Gall to the gates of hell to extract revenge. Fair enough?"

Will shook his head. "Guess I don't have a lot of choice right now."

CHAPTER 27

"Nothing yet," Henny hollered from his perch atop the rocks. He still had a piece of the little girl's dress sticking out of his trouser pocket. He took it out from time to time and sniffed it, as if reliving what he had done to her. "I'm getting mighty cold up here."

Justice looked at his younger brother and shook his head. Once they cleared the territory for warmer weather, Justice would leave Henny at some whorehouse and never look back. If he stayed out of a hangman's noose, it would be by his own hand. Justice had carried the kid along far enough. "Just keep your eyes glued to that spyglass."

"Maybe Ashley won't come."

"He'll come." *Damn fool,* he said under his breath.

"Of course, he'll come," Jack said. "He can't *not* come." Gall had tied Jack's wrists together with leather laces and roped him to a broken-off cottonwood laid over on the ground by a stiff wind. Jack squirmed to lessen the pressure on his hands, and blood spotted the snow from his severed finger. "I don't think I'd be so anxious to meet up with him."

"Anxious?" Justice looked over his shoulder at Jack. "I am giddy with the thought of finally meeting him face-to-face. And killing him slowly."

"What do you have against Tucker, except that he's managed to stay on your ass at every turn?"

Justice took off his mitten and stuck his hand under his

armpit beneath his coat to warm it. "Let's say we have a . . . history, Tucker Ashley and me. More importantly," he said, laughing, "is what's going to happen to you."

"You're going to put a bullet in my head before Tucker gets this far anyway."

"Maybe I'll let you live if Ashley gets within rifle range. Just as a reward for parting with your trigger finger."

Jack spat at Justice, but he was several yards short. "He'll come and slice your nose off for what your idiot brother done to Velma. And to the Swede's girl. He's driven by lining his sights up on your chest, not because he's worried about me."

Justice watched an eagle rise from the canyon behind the camp, a squirming coyote pup in its powerful talons. It disappeared down the next valley. "Just what *does* Tucker Ashley worry about?"

"Nothing."

Justice waved the air. "Every man worries about something."

"Okay. Here it is: he worries he might become just like you. He worries he'll start to enjoy the killing—"

"But it's too late—I understand he's done more than his share, if tall tales can be believed."

Jack nodded and wrapped his bandana tighter around his bloody hand. "He has, but last I knowed, he'd settled down. Aimed to marry that shopkeeper in Ft. Pierre." Jack grinned.

"Then why throw in with that posse? They're not exactly up to his caliber."

"My guess he just plumb missed the killing. Missing the chance to put a bullet into each and every one of you murdering bastards. Just like he done your farmer friend back in Hellion."

Justice's face flushed, and his fists balled up. He stepped toward Jack before he brought his temper under control. From what he knew of Tucker Ashley, Justice would need his wits about him. And losing it at the mention of Elias's death might doom him when Ashley finally came within his grasp.

Justice took off his hat as he stepped away from Jack. He waved the air, and from a hill higher than the rocks Henny sat on, Gall waved his hat in response. *No sign of Ashley yet.*

He turned back to Jack. "You're wondering why I don't kill you right now. If Ashley wants proof that you're still alive, I have to have a breathing, yelling-in-agony Jack Worman to prove you're still kicking." Justice waved away the notion that he'd kill Jack. "So, you see, I have to keep you breathing. At least until he's dead."

"Then at least give me another cup of that coffee."

Justice smiled. "I will, only because you seem to have a penchant for fine coffee. And because I am not a barbarian through and through, as the Wanted posters claim."

He poured Jack a cup from the pot hanging over the fire. He held the tin cup by the handle, the intense heat permeating the metal. He turned to Jack and squatted in front of him. "Careful, this is boiling hot. If a man were to toss it into another's face, it would surely disfigure that person." He handed Jack the cup but made no effort to step back.

"You're mighty trusting," Jack said. "With something this hot."

"It would serve you naught to scald me with the coffee. I'd recover and make your last moments a living hell. Besides, like I said before, I appreciate a man who enjoys a good cup of joe. And I make the best."

Jack grinned slightly. "It's the shits to be so predictable."

Justice stood and went to the fire. "And Ashley—is he as predictable?" Justice asked as he poured hot water from another pot into his cup. He untied a drawstring on his tea stash and sprinkled leaves over the top to steep. He drizzled snow into the hot liquid to cool it and savored the richness.

"Are you asking me if you'll be able to trap him?"

"That is what I am asking."

Jack laughed. "Not him. Just when you think you have him figured out, he does something totally unexpected. He might even have the back of your head in his sights now."

The hairs on Justice's neck stood erect, and he looked around so slowly that a man on a hillside might not detect the movement. He had witnessed how accurate Ashley could shoot with that buffalo gun of his, nearly drilling Gall that first night when the gang ambushed the posse. And few people had come that close to Gall Manahan, even during the war.

"And just when you thought you'd seen the last of him," Jack pressed his point, "he'll injun-up on you . . ."

"Justice!" Henny yelled, waving the piece of dress. "Two men riding here slow."

Justice set his cup down and scrambled up the dirt bank. Two men rode close enough that it looked as one rider at this distance. "Describe them."

Henny looked through the spyglass. "One's that gambler feller we sent after Ashley."

"And the other one?"

"He's in the lead."

"Dammit!" Justice hollered. "What the hell does the lead man look like?"

"Big feller," Henny said. "Got him one of those new Stetsons the folks been buying in the stores."

Justice cupped his hand and hollered, "Just tell me what he's riding."

Henny looked through the spyglass for a long moment before answering. "He's riding a big, goofy mule."

"That's him." Justice waved his hat across his face, and Gall responded. It would be the last time he'd see Gall until the shooting was over. When the former Confederate sharpshooter wanted to hide when he shot, there was no one who could spot him.

Justice waved Henny close, and he scrambled from his perch. "How far away are they?"

"Quarter, maybe a half mile."

"Good," Justice said. "Now repeat what you're supposed to do." He had never realized how much he missed Elias until Justice had given Henny a task.

"You don't want me to shoot Ashley."

"Good. What else?"

"I get up on those boulders. When they ride past that rock that looks kinda like a dog, I'm to start shooting at the other feller. But how's about if they're riding that close?"

"Then don't shoot at all unless Gall does. He's going to knock Ashley off his mule but not kill him."

"Where you gonna be?"

Justice pointed to a hill fifty yards past the boulders. "And you shoot from there." He motioned to other boulders.

"But I'll be the closet one to those fellers," Henny said. "Why am I the closest one? They might shoot me."

"That's a chance I'm willing to take," Justice said. "Besides, you're the worst shot among us. Now get on up there."

Henny was running toward the rocks when Justice stopped him. "And kid—you harm one hair of Ashley's head, it'll be yours next. When I mean leave that to Gall, I mean it."

Justice took off his coat and positioned his cartridge slide around his belt where he could grab fresh shells. When he finished, he took his bandana from around his neck and bent to Jack. He started to gag Jack with it, but he jerked away. "Thought you were a trusting man?"

"Not when my life depends on it," Justice said.

He grabbed Jack's head and held it still. He tied the bandana tightly around Jack's mouth. "Pardon my manners, but I can't take the chance that you'll holler out to the posse." He grinned. "This is better than my other idea—cut your tongue out so you won't warn them. You want that instead?"

Chapter 28

Tucker watched Pasqual and Will, riding Barney, approach from the east. Tucker had ridden around the backside where Pasqual said the Cauthers were camped. From the gambler's description, Tucker was certain he could locate it. But he knew that if he busted into the camp, Jack's life would be worth little. Nor would Will's or Pasqual's. As much as it pained him, Tucker knew he had to bide his time, find Gall and Justice, and kill them before they could harm Jack *or* the others.

"I still don't know about this," Will told him right before they headed out this morning. "Let's say Gall misses. Or, just as bad, wounds one of us. You only got one minute tops before he can reload and get back to shooting again."

"And when he shoots I'll know where he is. And that minute to reload? That'll give me time to kill Henny or Justice before firing on Gall."

"That's if they are fools enough to expose themselves."

Tucker was counting on his abilities, all right, with being able to shoot three times faster with his Sharps than Gall. Did he think Justice or Henny would show themselves?

"There's a reason no one's put a bead on Justice," Will said as he swung onto Barney's back.

Tucker had little argument for him. The Cauther gang had eluded everyone sent after them for a reason. Justice Cauther.

Tucker walked the last half mile, using a deep ravine to conceal his approach. From time to time he peeked over the rim until he came at a place where he could watch the valley and the approaching posse. And, more importantly, at a place where he could watch the tall butte that lorded over the lower hills.

Tucker low-crawled under a rotted log and rested the fore end of his Sharps between two branches. He would move before the shooting started, to a place with a clearer view of the butte, and he laid his shooting sticks beside the log. He had no illusions: he would have but a heartbeat to locate Gall when he fired that first round, and he needed to be as steady as he could.

He warmed his hands with his breath as he scoured the hills in front of him. Somewhere among the rocks and the hills situated above the rolling prairie the Cauther gang lay in ambush. Gall Manahan was surely situated on that tall butte, while Justice—or Henny—waited close to Jack. One of them would have to be close enough to kill him if necessary, a thought that made Tucker shudder.

Unless Jack was already dead. But Tucker didn't think so. He had learned things about Justice Cauther this last week, and one thing he discovered was the man planned for all events. He would keep Jack alive for a bargaining chip if things went south for the gang.

The sun glinted off something on top of a pile of boulders two hundred yards out. Tucker shielded his eyes with his hand and studied the rocks. Movement, faint, yet something fluttered with the wind. Tucker took out his binoculars and cupped his hand over the lens to prevent the sun reflecting from the glass. A small man—Henny Cauther by the description Pasqual had given—sat with his back against the rocks looking through a spyglass at the posse riding slowly toward his position. A piece of cloth dangling from Henny's back pocket waved with the breeze, as if begging for attention.

Tucker scanned the hills, looking for Gall Manahan, for that would be the one Tucker needed to kill first. With his Whitworth rifle, Gall could pick off the posse as far away as he could see them. But gauging from the way Gall had concealed himself that first night when the gang ambushed them, he would be most difficult to spot. Tucker's only hope was that Gall's first round was off, giving him time to spot where Gall hid. It was a long shot, in more ways than one.

Tucker silently cursed the Confederacy for training a sharpshooter like Gall Manahan, and for giving Tucker nightmares. Pinned down by southern marksmen at the disastrous Battle of Fredericksburg in '62, Tucker's Bucktail Rifles felt the south's fatal accuracy, killing from farther away than the Bucktails could see, until nighttime came and the survivors escaped. That afternoon it had become almost a personal game with Tucker—studying the terrain before him, the field of fire open to the Confederate sharpshooters—to figure out where the marksmen's hides were located. More often than not, Tucker was wrong. But the times he was right and surmised where the rifleman was concealed had saved his life. He was one of the few Bucktails to survive that day.

A small herd of pronghorns ran parallel with Will and Pasqual before veering away to safety. As Tucker looked out across the prairie with hills and hollows severe enough to conceal Gall, Tucker tried to guess—though he hated to stake Pasqual and Will's lives on a guess—just where Gall was hidden. Three different hills loomed high enough that they would give a good man with a rifle an excellent vantage point to fire from. Were the hills too far away? His Sharps .50 lacked the telescopic sight of Gall's rifle, but Tucker had used the Sharps enough, he was certain it was nearly as accurate. And a lot quicker to reload. That was his one advantage.

But Tucker wouldn't know where Gall was until he fired that first shot. Would his shot be a signal to Justice and Henny to start shooting? Tucker recalled the last ambush that first time they'd encountered the Cauthers, and the day Frank was murdered. Gall's first round would be a sign for the rest of the Cauthers to begin shooting. Tucker knew where Henny was: he'd ranged him at two hundred yards. Maybe two hundred proud. An unheard of shot for a Henry or Winchester. A normal shot for the Sharps. He was unsure of Henny's role in the ambush, but Tucker knew he could pick him off easily when the time came. He would have upwards of a minute before Gall could reload again once he fired. That minute would be Henny's downfall.

But which clump of rocks or sagebrush or scrub oak hid Justice? As he glassed the area with his binoculars, Tucker lost count of the many excellent ambush spots Justice could use.

Tucker blew dust off his peep sight and adjusted it for two hundred yards. He would wait until Gall fired before he took out Henny. Once Gall shot, Tucker would know just where he was hidden. And then there'd only be Justice Cauther left to kill.

As he breathed warm air onto his hands and watched the posse ride closer, Tucker was certain Justice Cauther's trigger finger was getting just as itchy as his.

Tucker backed away from the log and moved down the ravine twenty yards to where he could watch the butte better, trying but failing to spot Gall and Justice. The posse had ridden within five hundred yards of Henny, and Tucker wondered why Gall hadn't fired his first shot. Will kept his head lowered, and he bounced as he rode the mule, while Pasqual rode close to him as if his life depended on it.

Closer, now four hundred yards. And still Gall hadn't shot.

Tucker set the binoculars on the ground beside him and jammed his shooting sticks as far into the hard ground as they would go. He set the Sharps in the V and breathed onto his shooting hand to warm it once again. Gall *had* to shoot or the posse would soon be within rifle range of Henny's rifle . . .

. . . the glint of the sun, for the briefest moment, and Gall's shot echoed off the hills. The shot kicked up dirt inches in front of Will, and Barney hunched up.

Tucker lined his peep sight up on Henny. But not before he shot four quick rounds down range.

Pasqual dropped from his horse, his foot caught in the stirrup for the briefest time before he fell free into a clump of cactus. His roan ran across the prairie, blood smeared along the side of horse and saddle. Tucker marked in his mind Gall's position—where the puff of smoke filtered upward through rocks halfway down from the butte, a thousand yards perhaps.

Tucker focused on Henny as he took up slack on his rear trigger. He let his air out and gently tickled the hair, front trigger. The .50 knocked Henny from the rocks, and he rolled down onto the valley floor. He never cried out, never indicated he was in pain, for he'd died instantly, the bullet tearing a gaping hole through his coat, through his chest, visible even from Tucker's vantage point.

Will spurred the mule across for the safety of the rocks as bullets, fast and accurate, kicked up snow right behind him. Justice shot from somewhere Tucker couldn't see, and he opened the loading gate and shucked the spent cartridge out. He thumbed another big .50 into the chamber and hurriedly adjusted his peep sight for a thousand yards. He had settled behind the stock, digging his shooting sticks into the ground, when a slug tore up the ground in front of him. It hit his shooting sticks, splinters driving into Tucker's cheek as he saw another puff of smoke where Gall had shot the first time.

Gall made his first mistake—he had shot twice from the same place. Would he be so overconfident as to stay there and continue firing? Tucker shot toward the smoke and quickly dropped down from the rim of the gully.

He ran twenty yards along the trench before he scrambled up the bank to peer over. Black smoke still hung over where Gall fired. Tucker could envision the man hastily running another paper patch bullet on top of his powder charge, pushing a percussion cap on the nipple as he searched frantically for Tucker. For he must have realized the ruse. And Will became a low priority. Now Gall would concentrate on killing Tucker.

He took off Will's Montana Peak as he laid his Sharps against a sagebrush. He was vaguely aware that Will was returning fire, and that Justice was somewhere rapidly shooting back from somewhere on the far side of a hill to Tucker's left. But all that mattered to him was that he kill Gall Manahan. Everything else was secondary now. If he failed to kill the sharpshooter, his chances of saving Jack and Will were slim.

Tucker set the back trigger and lined his sights up where he thought Gall was hidden. Or had he moved when he realized Tucker spotted his smoke?

Tucker breathed deeply.

Let it out.

And flung Will's hat towards where he'd lain moments ago.

Gall's slug punched a neat hole in the hat even before it stopped rolling.

Tucker fired at the smoke.

He threw the loading lever, tossed another round in, and fired once more, ducking back into the coulee.

He scrambled another ten yards down and crawled high enough to see the hill Gall had staked out as his shooter's hide.

A glint of sunlight off a telescopic sight, another puff of smoke, another slow, deliberate shot that impacted where Tucker had lain a moment ago.

Tucker adjusted his aim a few inches down from where he'd

seen the glint of the scope.

And fired.

Recoil from the Sharps drove Tucker back several inches. When he brushed snow from his eyes, he saw a man on the side of the butte rolling down. The body stopped when it hit a scrub juniper growing on the side of the butte.

Gall Manahan was dead.

Tucker lay on his back, and for the first time in many years, he prayed—that he would be in time to save Jack—and he thanked God for sparing his life. The outcome could have been the opposite: Gall could have easily gotten the upper hand. And Tucker would now be lying on the frozen earth leaking his life blood onto the ground.

He became aware of shooting farther down the valley and looked over the rim of the ravine. Will fired as fast as his Winchester would operate at a man running across the prairie. Justice.

Tucker snapped a shot. His bullet kicked sage branches skyward in back of Justice as he dove behind some rocks. Tucker worked his way toward where Justice had disappeared, using the coulee as cover. A hundred yards away, perhaps as many as two; Tucker was uncertain. All he knew was that Justice ran *away* from where Pasqual said the gang kept Jack hostage.

Tucker reloaded. Soon Justice Cauther would go the way of John and Frank and Pasqual, Velma, and the Swede's little girl. Soon Tucker's Sharps would end the man's murderous spree when . . .

. . . . fading hoofbeats echoed off the rock formations.

Tucker scrambled up the bank, leading with his rifle, hoping to get one last shot.

But Justice had escaped.

Chapter 29

Tucker slung the Sharps and walked the last hundred yards to where Will lay reloading his rifle. He looked frantically around, ammunition dropping into the snow as he shook. Behind him Pasqual lay gut-shot, and another bullet had hit him low in his chest. Dark, frothy blood spewed from the gambler's mouth. Tucker knelt to him and pulled Pasqual's coat open.

"We get them?" Pasqual asked.

Tucker cradled Pasqual's head in his lap, and looked into the man's dying eyes. "We got them, boy."

Pasqual nodded once, and his breathing ceased.

Tucker eased his head onto the ground.

"Never had a chance." Will pointed to the tall butte. "Guess he gave his life for me, though he didn't know it. Gall's first shot went low." He looked sadly at Pasqual's body. "I figure Henny or Justice shot him." Will pulled Pasqual's hat over his lifeless eyes. "He said Jack is supposed to be over there," he pointed between two low hills. "At least that's the last thing he said before they ambushed us."

Tucker took Barney's reins, and he and Will headed between the two mounds of earth. "Some first posse I've been head of," Will said, his voice wavering. "That was the last man I've led, and now they're all dead." He stopped. "We need to bury Pasqual."

Tucker patted him on the back. "After we see to Jack."

They walked a few feet farther, and Will stopped. "I had this romantic notion of a posse hunting down killers—"

"We'll talk about it after we get back home. But for now, just remember—no posse has followed the Cauthers as long as we have." He jerked his thumb over his shoulder. "And every man knew the odds of signing up—"

Will shrugged Tucker's hand off his shoulder. "But none would have signed on if I'd been honest with them. They thought we were going after anyone beside the Cauthers."

"And when they found out the truth?" Tucker asked. "Even though they wanted to cut and run, in the end they all stuck it out."

Will shook his head. "I should thank you for killing Gall. His second shot might have found me."

"I got lucky, is all . . ." Tucker heard a muffled sound even before they stepped through the twin hills. Jack Worman lay beside a rotted tree, his hands bound just out of reach of the bandana tied tightly around his mouth. He tried speaking, but his lips were split, and his jaw swollen. He focused on Tucker through one swollen eye. The other closed completely as Tucker grabbed his Bowie and ran to Jack. Tucker dropped in the snow in front of Jack and cut him loose.

Jack tore the bandana from his mouth and spat blood onto the ground.

"Are you all right?" Tucker said for the third time before it registered with Jack.

He looked up at Tucker and Will as if seeing them for the first time. "I thought for sure I was a dead man. Sadistic bastard brother of Justice's kicked the hell outta me when I was tied up. When I get my hands on that—"

"For what it's worth, that sadistic little bastard is coyote food now." Tucker motioned where he'd shot Henny out of his perch. "And so is Gall Manahan."

"Justice?"

Will shook his head. "Got clean away. But you can track him, can't you?" he asked Tucker.

"If he can't, I can," Jack said, holding up his right hand. "He cut off my trigger finger." Jack was close to tears. "The son of a bitch cut my trigger finger off," and he started laughing.

"What's so funny?" Will asked.

"Jack shoots a pistol with his right hand," Tucker said. "But a rifle with his left. He can't shoot a pistol worth a damn, but he can still shoot a rifle as good as most men."

"And I will," Jack said. "Just set me on a horse."

"Which reminds me," Will said. "Where's mine? That mule of yours about beat me to a draw."

"Half a mile up that washout in back of here," Tucker answered. "I'll ride out in a minute and fetch him."

"Help me stand," Jack said.

Tucker offered Jack his hand, but he collapsed, holding his stomach. He wheezed heavily and grimaced with pain. "What the hell?"

"Henny kicked me a little too hard. Got some cracked ribs, I figure."

"Cracked, hell." Tucker motioned to the frothy blood Jack spat on the ground in front of him. "You might have a punctured lung." He turned to Will. "After I round up Pasqual's roan, I want you to tie Jack to the saddle, and you two light out. He needs a doctor—"

"I can ride."

"Like hell." Tucker gently helped Jack sit with his back against the tree. "Just this once, do as I say."

"You sound like you're leaving us."

Tucker chin-pointed in the direction Justice had fled. "I got to go after him."

"But with Marshal Dawes wet-nursing me to the nearest

sawbones," Jack said, "that means you'll have to go after Justice alone."

"Got no choice. Ain't come this far—and seen as many good men die—not to make sure the next one dead is Justice Cauther."

Will looked down at Tucker. "I don't know if that's wise—"

"I didn't say it was wise," Tucker said. "But Justice will get away if I don't. Your Appaloosa's in no shape to go much farther, and neither is Pasqual's roan. But my mule is just getting his second wind, and he'll need it with Justice riding one of the Swede's fresh mounts."

"Leave him be," Will said. "Nobody will blame us—we did our best to catch him."

"Would our best be good enough, remembering what they did to Velma and the Swede and his family—especially his little twelve-year-old girl? And don't forget your posse that's been systematically killed."

Tucker swung into the saddle and walked Barney toward where he had hobbled Will's Appaloosa. "Get Jack ready to ride. I'll fetch your horse and run down Pasqual's roan. As poor shape as your horses are in, they surely didn't run far."

"Where's the nearest doctor?"

"Might find one in Nowlin. If not there, make sure Jack gets somewhere he can get help.

"I told you—"

"And if you find an army patrol," Tucker said, ignoring Jack, "tell them what happened. You might luck out and find someone besides Captain Roush commanding the company."

"And tell them what, that we need help?"

"Tell them that Justice is headed for the Badlands, and I'm going after him."

Chapter 30

Justice rode fast away from the ambush site, making no attempt to hide his tracks, knowing Ashley would be able to follow him easily. He cursed himself as he rode down a deep coulee eroded by flash floods that often occurred there in the summer at the outskirts of the Badlands. Henny was dead, and so was Gall. Even though that left all the money to him, Justice wanted Ashley to suffer. It had always been about Ashley suffering, wasn't it?

He thought back to how each of his gang wanted to flee the territory. Go somewhere they could spend the money at their leisure. In hindsight, he almost wished he had agreed. But Justice had thought Tucker Ashley's scalp would be hanging from his saddle horn by now. He had grossly underestimated the man this past week, and especially when they had sprung the ambush an hour ago. Nothing could have gone wrong. Gall was hidden in a high place where he could fire down with impunity. Even the fool Henny was in a good spot to fire when the ambush was sprung. *Nothing* could have gone wrong. The last thing he suspected was the lead man wasn't Ashley, but that marshal. And that had cost Henny and Gall their lives.

Justice rode five hard miles before he stopped and dismounted long enough to hack off a large sagebrush. He looped his rope over it and trailed it behind, careful not to hide his tracks too well. He wanted to make it look as if he only hastily hid his tracks. He wanted Ashley to think he was a wounded animal after losing Gall and Henny. He wanted to be certain Ashley could follow him.

After a half mile, he stopped and stood in the stirrups. He snapped his spyglass open and eyed the way he had come. Rolling prairie could conceal a man and horse—or man and mule, in Ashley's case—or the rocks and boulders that became more prevalent the closer he rode to the Badlands.

He closed the spyglass, certain he wasn't followed yet.

To the west toward the Badlands the terrain became rockier, inhospitable, with more places where a man could hide. For someone like Justice, educated in the art of the ambush, the Badlands were the perfect spot to spring a trap on Ashley.

Justice had never ventured this far west—his hunting grounds were around the Missouri, south as far as Omaha, riding as far north as Bismarck. He had no desire to remain in the land of the Lakota any longer than necessary. He had seen too many squatters who had invaded this land only to meet dismal and dark ends at the hand of the Sioux. He would set a foolproof ambush for Ashley and ride far and fast as he could before *his* scalp was some Indian's trophy.

He surveyed the land ahead and glassed a rock formation a mile distant. Two tall spires, formed perhaps a million years ago when water flowed freely here, made a natural doorway, with a shallow gully running between them. He rode for it, judging the rocks to be twice as tall as a horse. More than high enough for his needs.

A herd of perhaps fifty buffalo rose from a washout and grazed what little grass remained. Justice paused, letting them pass. He wanted Ashley to follow him—he just didn't want him to so soon. And buffalo spooked and stampeding across the prairie would tell Ashley just where he was. *Let him work at it a little,* Justice said to himself. *I'm not going to make things any easier for you after the pain you caused me through the years.*

When the buffalo had moved on, Justice covered the last of the distance to the spires. He rode between them, dragging the sage by the ropes, obliterating his tracks. But not completely.

He looked for a place to hobble his horse. A hundred yards west in the direction of the Badlands he found it—a wash-out deep enough to hide a herd of horses. He hobbled the black's front legs and walked back to the stone doorway, his rifle slung over his shoulder, extra ammunition jingling in his pocket.

When he reached the sandstone spires, he climbed high on the rock to glass the area to the east. He saw nothing at first, until deer jumped from their resting spot and fled to the safety of another coulee. He kept his spyglass on the area where the deer spooked. A tiny speck along his back trail seemed to flicker, like an elusive winter mirage that shimmered and played tricks on his eyes. But the longer he looked at it, the closer it came. A man rode a horse. No—Justice clearly saw as the figures neared—a man approached riding a large mule. Unless Ashley and that marshal had traded mounts again, it was Tucker Ashley following.

Justice laid his rifle out on a rock and set a box of spare cartridges beside him. He began to shake with the anticipation of meeting Ashley face to face. He had killed Elias, his best friend—if a man on the run can have a best friend—and his sharpshooter whom he relied on for many years to keep posses off his back. And Ashley had killed Henny. Even though Justice often felt like slapping Henny senseless, he found himself missing the boy. Not because he was good company, or contributed to the success of their robberies, or possessed cunning, which one had to have to stay away from a hanging rope as long as they had. He missed Henny because he had been Justice's only kin. Ashley would rue the day he lived through Justice's ambush.

And for following his trail years ago.

★ ★ ★ ★ ★

When Justice sprang the ambush, it came almost too easily. Ashley was concentrating on the trail Justice had all but brushed clean, no doubt thinking he'd fled hell-bent-for-leather to get out of the territory as quickly as he could.

Ashley bent low over the saddle, studying the ground, easing the mule ahead at a brisk walk. As he rode between the two finger spires, Justice snapped two quick rounds, low to wound, his Winchester sounding as if he'd shot but once.

He levered another round in and stood to get another clean shot just as the mule went down. Blood spurted from a nasty chest wound, the animal's wailing bouncing off the rocks with a sickening sound. Ashley—trapped beneath the mule—struggled to free his leg.

Justice picked his way down the rocks. As Ashley clawed for his pistol, Justice shot again. The round bounced off the saddle and careened off a rock beside the mule.

"Don't even try to draw your gun."

Ashley held his hands well away from his holster as Justice approached him. He grabbed Ashley's pistol and tucked it inside his coat.

With a wink and a smile Justice snatched the Sharps from Tucker's scabbard. He ran his hand along the oiled stock. Hefted the gun and appreciated the craftsmanship. Admired the way in which Ashley had taken meticulous care of his rifle.

And swung it hard against a rock.

The stock shattered, and Justice flung it aside. "Shame that gun of yourn didn't survive," Justice said. "But not as much a shame as that mule of yourn. I'm not a betting man, but I'll wager he meant something to you."

Tucker stopped struggling. His leg remained trapped under the mule, and his other boot was stuck in the stirrup. "The least you can do is end his misery."

"I was just thinking the same thing," Justice said. "I hate to see a critter suffer." He drew an imaginary cross on the mule's forehead and pressed the barrel of his rifle against it. "I'd stay down for a second," he told Ashley and touched off his round. The mule's eyes bulged out from the concussive shock, and it settled onto the ground with a final snort.

Ashley tried pulling his leg out, but it remained trapped underneath. His boot still stuck in the stirrup, and Justice pulled it off Ashley's foot. "A little big for me," he held the boot up, "but I'll make do. Maybe I'll wear extra socks." He grinned. "Not a bad idea, as damnable cold out as it is."

"What the hell's your game?" Ashley said. "Just kill me and get it over with."

"I wouldn't dream of it." Justice walked behind Ashley and grabbed him by the coat collar. Justice set his legs and grunted and dragged Ashley clear of the mule. "The other boot," he motioned with his rifle. "Take it off. And shuck the coat as well. It's just about my size."

"So, that's your plan," Ashley said. "Leave me to freeze to death out here."

"Just lightening your load," Justice answered. "Now the belt. Unloose it and toss it over here. Wouldn't want you burdened down with something as heavy as a knife or holster."

Justice picked up Ashley's coat and gun belt and backed away. He felt in the pocket and found a handful of Lucifers. He tossed Ashley one of the matches. "Even I wouldn't be so inhuman as to leave someone out here in this weather with no heat. It's bad enough you got no coat. No boots. But with that match you'll be able to build a fire." Justice wagged a finger. "But use it wisely, old friend. Don't waste it just when a little chill overcomes you." Justice pulled his collar up against the wind and gave an exaggerated a shudder. "You might get into a real pickle and need the heat, but if you've already used the match for something trivial—"

"Like starting a fire."

Justice smiled. "You *do* understand your situation."

"Why not just kill me outright?"

Justice squatted in front of Ashley, and his gun remained leveled at his chest. "First off, you killed Elias Gates. My brother said some army sergeant got the drop on Elias and made him fight honest. Elias was a gunny, but nothing like the famous army scout Tucker Ashley. He knew a fair fight with the likes of you could only result in a bad ending for him."

"The son of a bitch was some brand of coward. He would have shot me with no chance for me to draw. Thank God for the army." Ashley laughed. "Did I mention I thoroughly enjoyed killing the bastard?"

Justice's temper began to rise, and he fought it back down. Ashley was trying to rile him. Make him err. Justice wanted neither. All he wanted was Ashley's last day to be his own personal hell. "And I won't kill you just because you killed Gall, though I don't fault you for that. Gall was mighty handy with that fancy target rifle of his." He chuckled. "Lord knows he enjoyed his work. Now that half-wit brother of mine is another matter—for as stupid and . . . crazy as he was, I still loved him. In my own way."

"Him I especially enjoyed seeing toppling from those rocks. Looked like he was in some kind of pain."

Justice felt his face flush, and he had stepped toward Ashley when he caught himself. "You'd like for me to get close."

"I'd love to get my hands around your filthy neck—"

"For the record—you get close enough to me to grab, and I'll give you a beating you'll never forget in the few short hours you have left before you freeze to death." Justice backed away, holding his rifle in one hand, Ashley's boots and coat in the other. "I hear tell there's some homesteaders squatted on land somewhere to the west. Not sure where exactly, but a resourceful feller like yourself might figure it out. You make it to them, and you might just survive."

Justice kept Ashley in his sight as walked toward his horse hobbled behind the cluster of rocks. "But watch your backside. I hear there's more than one Sioux war party loose hereabouts."

CHAPTER 31

Tucker picked his way around the rocks, using the oak branch he found as a makeshift walking stick to carefully step around sagebrush and sharp stones. His socks were rock-torn, with blood seeping through where he'd cut his feet, thankfully numb from the freezing temperature. The frigid wind whipped through his shirt, and he wrapped his arms around himself to try to stymie the cold.

He tried following Justice's tracks, but fresh snow—whipped into a frenzy by stiff winds blowing off the Badlands—obliterated any sign he left. But right now, where Justice rode mattered less to Tucker than his own survival. He shivered violently from the onset of hypothermia, and he stumbled across the ground on feet suffering from frostbite. Only with the aid of the walking stick did he maintain his balance. If he didn't find some shelter soon, he'd be dead by morning.

He fidgeted in his vest pocket to reassure himself the match was still there. Though he desperately needed to start a fire, Justice had been right: Tucker had better save that one Lucifer for when his life depended on it. He wasn't there yet, but he was close.

He squatted with his back against a boulder as much out of the wind as he could get. Snow swirled overhead, and he gathered his shirt collar tighter around his neck. The intense cold numbed his limbs, causing them not to function as they should, and his head bobbed on his chest. He fought sleep and shook his head to clear it. Everything he did now was done slowly, as if rushing movement would cause his body to snap from the freezing temperature much like a pump jack did on some very cold mornings.

Even his thoughts came to him slowly, painfully. How long had it been since Justice set him afoot? A half day? More? What stuck in Tucker's mind the most was that Justice really didn't miss his gang as much as one would have thought. So, what drove the man to hate Tucker so much?

His head dropped onto his chest once again.

He told himself to stay awake; that if he dozed, death would quickly visit him.

He would close his eyes. Just for a moment, he promised himself. And he would start again.

He awoke with pain radiating all the way down his legs and feet. How long he'd slept, he was unsure, but snow partially covered him. He looked down at his feet. An inch of fresh powder covered his socks, blending them in with the ground.

Something had awakened him from what might have been his last sleep, but what? As he rested against the rock too cold to move, he became aware of sounds drifting toward him with the shifting of the wind. A rider—or riders—rode close, their horses snorting protest, as if wanting to get away from this place of cold rocks and windswept ground.

Tucker grabbed on to his walking stick and stood painfully. He kept his head immobile and looked to his side. In his periphery, he caught movement, heard the whinny of an impatient pony. Two Lakota warriors studied the ground. They spoke among themselves, but Tucker couldn't understand what they said over the wind.

And they would pass within a few feet of where he stood half-covered in snow.

He wanted to, needed to, stomp his feet to regain some

circulation, but he dared not. His legs seemed frozen to the ground, and he had lost feeling in his feet. The wind nearly toppled him, and he clung tightly to his oak branch.

The Indians neared, confused as they watched the ground beneath them, and it became obvious they tracked Tucker, and also obvious they had lost him in this storm.

Another few feet and they would see him. But what were they doing out in a snowstorm after him? Recognition overcame Tucker's dulled senses—these were the last two Lakota from the raiding party. One Indian had tied his light-brown hair in a single horse tail at the back of his head, while the other wore his black braids down his chest, tucked under the blanket around his shoulders. At the last fight where the older Indian had been killed, Tucker thought these two would break off the stalk and return to their village. He had underestimated the pair, perhaps because they were the youngest warriors. And would have something to prove to their tribe.

He thought hard to clear his mind, frantically planning how he would react if they looked his way. Both young men were probably on their first raiding party away from their tribe. Trade blankets were wrapped tightly around their thin shoulders, and Tucker estimated them to be smaller than Jack. If he could get within grabbing distance, that might be his only advantage. If there could be any advantage with the Sioux.

Tucker flexed his fingers, but they didn't flex so well, and he had to force them open. He closed his hand tighter around the oak branch and flattened himself against the depression in the rock face.

He willed his breathing to slow, as . . .

They cleared the edge of the rocks where Tucker hid, passing within feet of him. They were riding single file, studying the ground intently, neither looking his way when . . .

. . . the braided warrior pulled his pony up short. The lead man with the horse tail braid continued on, oblivious to his friend's stopping. He sniffed the air as he looked around.

Then his gaze fell on Tucker. He did not immediately registerwhat he saw, the suddenness of finding the man they were trailing causing shock in the young man's eyes. And, in that second when uncertainty and surprise overcame the Indian, Tucker swung the walking stick. It hit the man in the shoulders and knocked him off his horse.

Tucker screamed and flailed the air with his stick.

The pony reared up, and Tucker grabbed for the reins.

The horsehair hackamore slipped from his frozen grasp, and the pony bolted across the prairie as the lead man turned in his saddle. He turned his horse but pulled up short when the Indian Tucker had knocked to the ground jumped up. He threw his blanket off his shoulders and drew his knife. He lunged at Tucker, but the attack was that of an inexperienced warrior, and he came too close to his prey.

Tucker jabbed with his stick, and the blow landed flush on the Indian's face. He blinked in disbelief as blood poured from a shattered nose. Tucker smashed the branch down on his hand, and the knife dropped from his hand.

Tucker stepped closer and swung again, but the warrior leapt back. He lost his balance and fell to the ground. By the time the lead warrior had turned his pony back to help his friend, Tucker had picked up the knife. He screamed as he shuffled toward the injured Indian, slashing with the knife in one hand, the stick in the other.

The Sioux was struggling to get to his feet, unable to focus through his bloodied eyes, when the lead Indian reached down and swung the man onto his pony. Tucker hobbled after them on bloody and near-frozen feet, lashing the air with the knife. The last thing he saw was both Indians galloping away, looking back as if seeing the ghost of a white man ready to follow them into hell.

Tucker picked up the blanket and wrapped it around his shivering shoulders. The trade cloth was thin and barely covered him, but he was grateful for anything that would break the wind and gain him some relief from the cold.

He tucked the knife into his trousers and looked after the Indians. They galloped across the prairie, looking back, until they were but a speck of movement in the snow. His greatest fear was that other Lakota were close. Would the two young Indians admit to the big bellies, the old and wise men of the tribe, that an unarmed *wasicu* had put the run on them? Perhaps not, yet Tucker knew that at any moment more Lakota would ride in search of him. And he knew he needed to get away from this place.

Some time later, as the sun was overhead, teasing, cruelly withholding its heat, Tucker stumbled in deep snow, his walking stick buried halfway up the shaft with every step. Around every boulder, nearing every gully deep enough to conceal men and ponies, he prepared for another assault, clutching the knife as if he could ward off a full Sioux war party. He tripped over whitened buffalo bones partially buried in the snow. He tumbled down a hill, and the blanket shredded as it grazed against sharp rocks. He managed to retain hold of the knife only because his fingers were too cold to snap open when it broke his fall.

He thrust his walking stick into the clump of gramma grass that had stopped him. He tried standing, but he fell back and caught his breath. Drops of blood formed in the snow from a gash on his head—compliments of a sandstone outcropping halfway down the hill. *At least if I'm bleeding I'm alive,* he thought.

He tried standing again but fell back to the ground. His

breath came in wheezing gasps, and he blew air into his cupped hands while he looked around him. To one side, underneath a rock outcropping, was a depression clear of snow deep enough that he could lie down and have some relief from the biting wind. He was crawling toward it when he spotted fresh rabbit tracks. He followed the tracks as they paralleled the rocks; a game trail that the rabbits used to weave their way among the stones.

Tucker cut strips off the tail of his shirt. He fashioned two snares and set the loops to both sides of the trail, where the rabbits ran between two large rocks. Finished, he shuffled back up the hillside to the depression under the outcropping and lay flat. Snow fell around him, over him, but the wind carried the powder past him in swirling eddies.

He curled in a fetal position and gathered the blanket—sliced and holey from the rocks—around his trembling shoulders. He shook his head to stay awake. He dared not doze, yet the cold was so intense. He felt the match in his pocket and considered using it, his mind playing tricks of a roaring fire before him.

And his eyes closed.

When he awoke hours later, snow had partially covered him. He gathered his legs under him and stood, shaking the snow off. His trouser legs were as stiff as a saddle, and ice had formed on his week-old beard. He was standing on wobbly legs when movement down the hill caught his eye. Two rabbits thrashed around, squealing as they fought his snares.

He hobbled as fast as a bootless man could and dropped beside the rabbits.

A quick twist of their necks, and Tucker freed the loops around their heads. He gutted them and started back toward his depression among the rocks, picking up twigs and sage branches sticking out of the snow as he went.

He laid the twigs in a pile and covered them with larger

cottonwood branches he'd gathered. His hand trembled as he brought the Lucifer from his pocket. He was bending to the branches to blow on the kindling once the match was lit, when he felt someone close by.

He sat up slowly, wrapping his hand around the knife, feeling his oak stick lying beside him. He expected the Indians to have come back for a rematch, when he spotted Justice Cauther thirty yards downhill. He sat his horse with one leg thrown over the saddle horn. He cupped his hands around a match and lit a smoke. He grinned while he looked at the match for long moments before blowing it out. "Bet y'all wish you had more of those. But you don't. You got just that one match."

Tucker's grip tightened on the knife hidden in his hand under the snow. Even if he was limber enough, Tucker wouldn't have been able to reach Justice before he drew and fired. "I thought you'd be enjoying your money in Mexico by now."

Justice blew smoke rings that the wind quickly carried away. "Was a time that's all I wanted—to enjoy my money while I warmed these bones on some sunny beach. Have some lovely *senoritas* wait on me. But that's not what I enjoy nowadays. You know what I enjoy?"

Tucker hugged the blanket tighter. "No, but I'm sure you'll tell me."

The smile left Justice's face, and a fierce expression overcame him. His lip curled as he spoke, and his fist balled up. "What I enjoy most is seeing you eke one more day from your miserable life. One more day of wondering if you'll see another sunrise." He nodded to the rabbits. "But I see you're even more resourceful than I imagined a Yankee to be."

"And a Yankee who killed your brother, and those cowardly bastards you rode with—"

"Don't bring them up again—"

"Or you'll what—kill me?" Tucker forced a laugh as his hand

tightened around the knife. "But makes no difference what side I fought for. Didn't anyone tell you the war's over?"

"It'll never be over for you and me."

"What the hell does that mean?"

"You think about it while you're freezing your ass off." Justice chuckled. And he nodded to Tucker. "I see you got you some ratty blanket that might take some of the edge off." He jerked his thumb over his shoulder. "I'm betting those Indians will be coming back with help to reclaim their property any time now."

"Is that what you came to tell me?" Tucker's teeth chattered so forcefully he thought he'd chip them.

"I came to give you a friendly reminder—"

"So, you've been close, watching me all this time?"

"—that if you use that Lucifer and cook those bunnies, you won't be able to save yourself when the temperature drops even colder." He turned his head skyward. "And it looks like a front's coming in."

"And you want me to live as long as possible, is that it?"

"I want you to *suffer* as long as possible." Justice unhooked his leg from the saddle horn and started riding slowly across the broken prairie. "But suit yourself," he called over his shoulder, his voice nearly lost to the wind. "Y'all use that match now, and I doubt we'll talk in this world again."

Tucker shivered violently as he watched Justice ride out of sight. He desperately wanted to use the Lucifer—not only to roast the rabbits, but to start a fire that would help his system return to the living.

He looked once more at his match and pocketed it inside his vest. Justice was right again. There might be a time tomorrow—or the next day, *if* he survived—when he might need a fire even more than he did now. And the thing that drove him was meeting Justice one more time when he was able to kill him properly.

He picked up one of the rabbits and—being hungrier than he was civilized at this moment—began eating them raw.

A tumbleweed driven by the fierce wind rolled into Tucker, and he woke from a fitful sleep. He batted his arms to shake off his grogginess and flexed his feet. He needed to get circulation back, and he dug his walking stick into the snow and stood.

He pulled the blanket tight around him and studied the storm clouds. It had begun snowing heavily while he slept. He shook snow off the blanket, heavy and wet from this recent dump, and he patted snow off his trousers.

Tucker squinted against the blinding whiteness reflecting off the snow and scoured the terrain. Justice was out there somewhere. Watching. Tucker had grown to know the killer well these past days, and he knew Justice was close enough that he could keep an eye on Tucker. Out there. Somewhere.

Tucker needed to stand. But Justice had no intention of leaving until he had personally witnessed Tucker's painful agony leading to the slow death that was creeping up on him. How long he had before the elements turned him into stone only to be melted come spring, he didn't know. All he knew was that if it looked to Justice that Tucker might actually live through this ordeal, the man would swoop in and kill him.

But Tucker's rage had grown and festered like a boil under a saddle since Justice left him afoot to freeze—it was the only emotion that broke through his dulled senses. He had no intention of giving Justice the satisfaction of lying down and dying.

The rabbit had nearly frozen during the hours after the kill, and Tucker gnawed on it until all that remained was bone and gristle.

He turned his back against the pelting sleet and snow. He watched the storm front with concern. To the west, the clouds were heavy and dark and ominous, with the potential of dropping enough snow to completely cover him if he dozed off again. The winds driving the clouds portended a blizzard that would bury everything in its path.

But Justice would also see it, and he would seek out a sanctuary to weather the storm. Suddenly, pent-up rage against the man broke through Tucker's clouded mind as he realized this storm might be his salvation. That wonderful blizzard just might save him.

He sucked the marrow out of the bones before tossing them aside and turning to the two hides lying at the lip of his shallow depression. After he had skinned them, he rubbed snow on the fur side to wash the blood off and used the Indian's knife to scrape the inside free of fat. He slapped the hides against a rock before he turned them inside out.

He wiped the knife on his trousers and cut thin strips from the tattered blanket. He braided three strips for each rabbit hide and lashed the fur to his feet. He stood and tested his new shoes. The rabbit fur felt like he was walking on soft moss. They weren't boots, but they helped insulate his feet from the snow and sage and sharp rocks that had torn the skin off his feet.

He sat back in his depression in the ground, certain that Justice was out there watching him with the captain's glass Tucker had seen dangling from his saddle horn. But that was all right—he expected Justice to be holed up where he could watch Tucker. But how long before the storm hit?

Tucker settled back and wrapped what remained of the blanket around his shoulders. He had eaten, though it had been a raw meal, and he scooped snow to melt down his parched throat. And with a seed of a plan growing in his mind, he was glad now he hadn't wasted the match on the rabbits.

Where was Justice? Tucker had no idea as he looked to the west. He could not see where a man might hide. Hell, he couldn't even see the land for the whiteness, and it was getting worse. But he knew the terrain became much rougher four or files miles west, the rocks and the coulees higher and deeper, the closer to the Badlands one travelled.

As he looked to the storm clouds, he knew it was a matter of only a few hours before the snow would dump on him mightily. He had seen such storms deposit a foot of snow in mere hours.

For the first time in days, he smiled. He was counting on that beautiful blizzard.

Chapter 32

Justice awoke to a coyote howling at the morning sun peeking between low-hanging snow clouds. He threw the tarp, heavy with snow, off his bedroll and sat up. The storm came and went with a scream as it headed toward the river town miles to the east, and it had subsided to a gentle breeze that swirled fresh snow around him. Last night before he covered himself up against the blizzard, he'd had the forethought to gather firewood and cover that over as well. If he'd learned nothing else from his drunk-of-a-daddy—and something he'd tried to teach his stupid half brother when he was alive—was that a man ought to begin each day with dry firewood.

He dug his bag of tea leaves and water pot from his saddlebags and scooped snow into the pot. He carefully laid out firewood over kindling of broken juniper branches, careful because he could be careful. Careful, because he wanted to take his time making Ashley suffer just a little more, while Justice enjoyed a hot cup of tea. But with the blizzard coming on as wickedly as it had last night, he would be astonished if Ashley were alive this morning.

While the fire caught, he took a sack of jerky from inside his shirt. He set a log close to the fire as he placed the water pot on the coals to boil. Soon, he told himself, he would never have to worry if he had dry firewood, for in Mexico all wood was dry. He wouldn't have to worry about his next meal being pieces of fatty jerky stolen from a trader town along the Missouri. He would live well on the money in his saddlebags; he would order beans and tortillas the night before from a lovely *senorita* paid to keep him happy all night and serve him breakfast the next morning. He would hire *peones* happy to serve their *patron* with whatever he wished. He would look back at this time—living in this freezing, barren land—as a mere bump in his life. Just as soon as he was certain Ashley had suffered enough. And when he had, Justice would sit on a sandy beach and toast Henny and Gall and Elias for helping him get there.

He sprinkled tea leaves over the top of the hot water and set his cup close. While the tea steeped, he grabbed his spyglass from the saddle next to his bedroll and extended the long tube. It took him a moment to spot where Ashley had lain in his depression in the ground like some animal, the snow making the landscape look all the same.

Justice saw the sandstone outcropping he used for a marker to spot Ashley's whereabouts and followed it down a few feet.

And he jerked the spyglass away.

He rubbed the sleep out of his eyes and looked again. Unless he had the wrong outcropping—things often looked different from a thousand yards away . . . No, he had the right spot at the base of the rocks. Ashley was either buried and dead before Justice wanted him to be . . .

Or he had escaped during the blizzard.

Justice hastily downed his cup of tea before he paused and breathed deeply to calm himself. Ashley wasn't gone. No man dressed with nothing more than a blanket and rabbit skins for shoes could have made it through that storm.

He was buried. By the looks of the snow on Justice's tarp this morning, the blizzard had dumped nearly a foot of snow overnight. And given the wind that had awakened him with a howling vengeance a couple of times, much more snow might have drifted into Ashley's depression in the ground.

Justice finished the last of his tea and packed up his camp. When he stood to saddle his horse, he looked again where he'd left Ashley, cold and hungry and without any fire to stave off the freezing temperatures. He couldn't have escaped—the snow *had* covered his frozen corpse sometime during the night.

Justice broke camp and saddled the black. It tried to nip him, the gelding's teeth clattering as if the Swede himself were inside the horse seeking revenge. Justice stayed just out of the range of the black's mouth as he mounted him and coaxed the animal down the steep hillside. He rode past a shivering scrub juniper that barely kept rooted against the wind and arrived at the outcropping under which Ashley lay buried. The depression was no more—the snow had made the area as flat as the tall-grass prairie he preferred to this barren death trap.

Justice grabbed the small shovel hanging from his saddle and dismounted. He began probing the ground until he found an area—Ashley's last bed—covered over. Justice dropped to his knees and frantically scooped away the snow.

Ashley *was* gone.

Sometime during the night, he had wandered away from the safety of his hole in the ground. But how could a man with so little protection from the cold go very far?

Justice stood and grabbed his spyglass once again. He searched the rolling hills, every clump of grass that had sprung up on a hillside, every rock formation big enough to hide someone of Ashley's bulk. He saw nothing, and any tracks Ashley might have left were under nearly a foot of snow.

Justice mounted his horse and stood in the stirrups. He had glassed all about him when . . .

. . . a thin tendril of smoke appeared to the west toward the Badlands. Just one small puff that was quickly taken away by the wind. Justice brought the spyglass away and rubbed his eyes. When he looked back, he spotted another brief line of smoke rising, perhaps more than two miles away.

He smiled and looped the glass over his saddle horn. So, Ashley had made it that far. Justice once again found himself admiring the man, even though he knew he must kill him in the end. In another life, he and Ashley might have ridden the trail together, fattening their pockets, trusting one another to watch their backs.

In another life.

In this life, Justice told himself, he'd soon kill Tucker Ashley.

Justice had never been this far west, never been to the Badlands. Even though he feared no man, he knew a man was a fool not to hedge his bet and stay out of the Sioux homeland. He'd always thought entering the land of Lakota—right where the Badlands were situated—would have been foolish, even with the rest of his gang with him. It might prove to be absolutely crazy now for him to go into the Badlands by himself. Especially now that Ashley had started a fire. If Justice spotted it, the Indians certainly would.

Mexico sounded so appealing to him, and he turned his gelding to the south when he stopped. As much as he wanted that warm, sandy beach to engulf him and ease all his tensions, he wanted Tucker Ashley at the end of his sights more.

Chapter 33

As Tucker walked bent over against the wind, barely keeping erect with the aid of his walking stick, he questioned the wisdom of leaving the relative safety of his hole in the ground. Though it was nighttime, stars and the moon backlit the whiteness on the ground, and he had easily picked his way west.

Until he became confused and lost. He had become lost once when he went deer hunting in Pennsylvania as a boy. He had wandered in circles, each tree looking just like all the others, no landmark that he foolishly thought he knew standing out. But in the morning, his father and a group of men from the church found him cold and alone, hugging a maple tree. His father wouldn't be coming to help him this time.

He stomped his feet and flapped his arms, but nothing relieved his violent trembling. Had he walked in circles as he had as a boy? That rock formation looked like one he might have passed an hour ago. There was a stand of scrub oak that looked like one he had seen someplace within the last hour. Perhaps right here, when he'd passed it before. He was unsure, and he was confused. He needed to get his bearings, yet nothing he did helped. He was totally and completely lost.

Until he came upon a lone buffalo bull.

Tucker thought it another hallucination until it lowered its great ice-covered head and snorted loudly before continuing on its way. If the buffalo knew a man stumbled within yards of him, it gave no indication. But then, few things offered such an enormous beast any danger—and a half-frozen and unarmed man wasn't one of them.

The buffalo kept its head lowered as it plodded through the deep snow. Tucker followed, though he didn't know exactly which way they went. Sometime during the night the realization filtered through his foggy brain—buffalo are smart. A lot smarter than cows, especially out here in the prairie. Cows walked with the storm, figuring they could get away from the menacing wind and snow. But in the end, they spent more time fighting the blizzard.

Buffalo walked into the wind, knowing that was the quickest way to get through the storm and on with their lives. Tucker lost sight of the buffalo bull when the wind started dying down. But not before the beast had saved his life. In its own way.

Tucker lay under the blanket of snow, his eyes the only thing Justice would see if he looked this way. The fire crackled and blazed thirty feet away, and more than once Tucker had debated whether or not to crawl over to it and thaw himself out. But to follow through with his only chance at Justice, he must keep hidden. That Justice would spot the fire and come on the run, Tucker had no doubt—he had built up the fire high and hot enough that a man with a spyglass could easily see him.

Or an Indian spotting a strange fire in his land. And that worried him even more than the thought of Justice Cauther.

The last thing on his mind last night when he had trudged through the blizzard had been those two Lakota he had frightened away. If they were too proud to tell the Big Bellies they had been bested by an unarmed white man, no other Indian would come looking. If they swallowed their pride and admitted a *wasicu* had beaten one and put the run on both of them, more would come looking for Tucker. He shuddered—not merely from the cold—but from what he knew the Sioux would do to a white man they found trespassing on their land.

He recalled what Justice told him about the homesteaders along the rim of the Badlands that he thought might help Tucker. Justice had his stories right—but he was a year too late on the outcome. Three homesteaders had been foolish enough to stake out land in Sioux hunting ground. Then last year, they'd been wiped out, with the army left riding in circles looking for an enemy they would never find. There were no homesteaders here to help him now. Not the army either. Especially with the ever-brave Captain Roush patrolling close to towns with wild saloons.

He would have to save himself.

But wasn't that how it always was? During the war, company commanders called upon him more for his tracking abilities than for his fighting spirit, especially when they looked for cross-border Confederate raiders. The last time he accompanied a Union hunting party, they had tracked a lieutenant of Bloody Bill Anderson's to a Kansas saloon. The captain had dismissed Tucker before he could revel in the capture. The captain had sent Tucker back to his unit, only to be captured and spend the rest of the war in a Confederate prison. He hadn't been successful on his own then. But he vowed he would be this time. Justice was at stake.

After he found this ambush spot, he cut more strips from the blanket and lashed the knife to his walking stick. As he settled in to allow the snow to cover him until he could spring the ambush, the thought of driving his makeshift spear into Justice Cauther motivated him to stay awake.

Movement caught his eye—movement that could easily have been in his mind's eye only. A man on the brink of freezing often sees things that aren't there—like a mirage across a painted desert during a dry summer.

Again something moved to one side of him, and he turned

his head as far as he could without disrupting the snow. A lone man on horseback rode toward him. A careful man. A man expecting someone to leap on him from the rocks high overhead, or from a drifted-in buffalo wallow that dotted the Badlands. Justice sat his horse, looking from the smoke to the ground, trying to pick up Tucker's sign. But Tucker had walked here during the night, the blizzard covering any sign he might have left, and he was certain Justice would not spot his tracks. And couldn't spot Tucker, even if he stood from his high vantage point.

And another movement, the faint flicker of a horse's tail approaching from the other direction. A paint pony rode over a far ridge a half mile away. Three other men on ponies rode single file behind him. As they neared, Tucker saw that one Indian's face was covered with a bandage of some sort—the young warrior whom he had hit with his stick and broken his nose. Broken Nose pulled up the rear, following his friend of two days ago. In the lead were two older warriors. One held a rifle across his lap; the other, a war bow. As they approached Tucker's blazing fire, he notched an arrow.

Only a wide butte separated them from the path Justice took. The Indians hadn't spotted Justice yet. But they soon would and would probably kill Justice, though the man had survived this long. His demise wasn't a sure thing. Discounting the inexperienced warriors Tucker had fought two days ago, the lead Indians looked hardened by years of hunting, years of combat against whomever crossed their paths. If they surprised Justice, he would have no chance. He would be dead.

Then the Indians would come to see who had started a fire, and they would find Tucker.

If they killed Justice, Tucker would have to fight four men armed only with a makeshift spear. Against four Lakota warriors he had no chance. Against Justice, Tucker might be able to set a trap for him. He would have stood a good chance of surprising him from the hole Tucker hid in all night. Now he would have to leave the relative safety of his hole and set an ambush some other place.

As soon as he alerted Justice.

As much as it pained him, he'd have to help Justice survive the Lakota attack. Besides, he so wanted to kill Justice himself. For Velma and the Swede's little girl.

Tucker backed up in the snow, using the blanket to obliterate his tracks, keeping low so as to stay behind the rocks in front of him. The rabbit skin shoes had provided his feet some protection, but the rest of his body ached from the deepest cold he ever recalled, and he shivered violently. Even covering his tracks with the blanket took energy, and he sat on a downed cottonwood while he surveyed the terrain. The war party had made their way around a field of sage littered with sharp rocks and cactus. Tucker estimated they'd emerge from the far side of the butte within minutes and spot Justice riding in the open.

Justice rode slowly, still eying the ground, but the Indians would see him first and set an ambush. Minutes. That was all Tucker had to climb higher on this boulder pile where he could warn Justice without getting himself shot. It was a ploy he wasn't sure he could pull off.

Justice kept watching the ground ahead as he rode, now a hundred yards away from the fire. Ashley had finally come so close to freezing to death, he'd used the Lucifer. He didn't blame the man—Justice was certain he would have used the match long ago. But it didn't matter to him now. As soon as he found Ashley, he would kill him and head south like he should have done days ago.

He kept watching the ground, but no tracks emerged. Ashley must have walked away from that shallow depression where he'd been at the start of the blizzard, for the snow had covered his tracks completely. Ashley himself was covered over with snow somewhere. Justice would find him. Or the black would. Justice would simply ride through the snow around the fire until the horse stepped on the man buried in the snow. Would Ashley still be alive? Justice doubted it. Even if he survived the blizzard and managed to start a fire, it would be too late. He'd be as frozen as a stock pond in January.

His horse's ears twitched, and the animal snorted once. Justice stopped thirty yards from the fire and studied his horse. The animal's attention was drawn to a butte perhaps a hundred yards wide on the far side of the fire. The butte flowed naturally into boulders a few yards to one side. The rocks seemed to have been piled randomly by some great ancient flood. There were open spaces beside other rocks packed tighter than a man could walk through. A man could hide among those boulders, but he doubted Ashley was there; the man was buried and dead by now. Still, it hadn't been that long ago that Ashley had started the blaze.

Justice watched and waited, but nothing stirred. He coaxed the gelding closer to the fire.

Suddenly someone screamed. The horse bucked and sunfished as Justice fought the reins to stay in the saddle as another yell rose and echoed off the rocks ahead.

Tucker Ashley stood on a rock ledge ten feet up. He waved his arms wildly and hollered.

Justice levered a round into his rifle as a Lakota spurred his horse from behind a boulder. The pony struggled in the foot-deep snow, and the Lakota snapped a shot with his Henry. The shot went wild as another Sioux riding behind him launched an arrow that clipped Justice's shoulder.

He felt the arrow take out a piece of flesh as it pierced his coat and penetrated the front of his jacket, right before he fired his rifle. His bullet shattered the Indian's jaw, and blood spurted out his wound as he fell onto the fresh powder.

Two more Lakota kicked their ponies' flanks, riding straight at him. Justice hip-shot. Missed.

The Indian with the rifle dropped it when he crashed his horse into Justice. He snatched a knife from his waist and slashed at Justice's face. The Indian's blade ripped the side of Justice's neck, and he jerked his head back. The warrior was drawing his knife back when Justice grabbed his leg and pulled him off the horse. He drove his fist into the Indian's face, shattering bones, knocking him down. He struggled to stand in the deep snow. Blood spurted from a broken nose, and he wiped blood out of his eyes.

Justice stumbled back and lost his balance in the snow. He gathered his legs under him as the two young Indians rode for him. Justice stood on shaky legs, clawing for his pistol under his coat as one of the young Lakota sighted down the shaft of his arrow.

A blur from the rocks came then, as Ashley leapt from his place on the ledge. He swung a long stick that crashed down on the young Indian's back. His arrow launched wildly over Justice's head.

Ashley wrestled with the Sioux—younger and stronger now that Ashley was nearly frozen and covered with snow. They fell to the ground, rolling, both struggling to gain the upper hand.

The Indian drew his knife and brought it down in a lazy arc at Ashley's chest. He blocked the knife with his arm. The Sioux kicked him in the groin, but Tucker felt little pain in his frozen body, and he grabbed the warrior in a bear hug as they rolled across the snow.

He got the Indian in a choke hold and wrapped his legs around the man's torso as he sat back on the ground, tightening the hold. In moments, the young warrior ceased breathing, and

Tucker lay back, sucking in air, still holding the Indian's body.

Justice squatted behind rocks and peeked around them as he drew his Colt. The Indian he'd fought with had regained his footing—and his rifle—and dove behind thick sagebrush, firing his rifle as he went.

The other young Sioux with the bandage across his nose stood from behind a pile of rocks, clutching a knife. He screamed and rushed Justice.

The Indian behind the sagebrush yelled something in Lakota, but the man ignored him. Justice let him get within feet before shooting him twice in the chest.

Justice ducked back behind the rocks. Rifle rounds kicked chipped rocks into his eyes, and he wiped them away while he thumbed fresh cartridges into his Colt.

Just as hoofbeats faded quickly away.

Justice fired three rounds into the sage to keep the Indian's head down and looked at the horse riding away. He saw a white man riding hell bent for election, holding a long pole. He steadied his pistol on the top of the rock and fired. The horse hunched once before it disappeared down a deep ravine.

And Justice knew he needed to quickly kill the last Indian standing between him and Tucker Ashley.

CHAPTER 34

Justice found the black grazing on some gramma grass a quarter mile from the ambush scene. If the Indians knew about the money sitting in the bottom of his saddlebags, they might have broken off the attack and stolen his take. But, no; they wouldn't have. They cared little about white man's money or the methods of acquiring it. All they thought about was territorial power, and killing anyone who crossed their paths. Just like he felt about Tucker Ashley right now.

He grabbed the reins and began following the blood trail left by the wounded horse. He rode the black atop a hill overlooking a vast valley and snapped open his spyglass. A speck on the horizon to the east caught his eye. He stood in the stirrups and stared through the glass. Jack Worman rode bent low in the saddle studying the ground, one arm holding his ribs where Henny had kicked him. He was perhaps a mile back, following Justice. He'd made no attempt to hide his back trail—there was no need, for his prey lay in front of him. But Justice had no need to worry—Worman was probably as trail beat as Ashley. And with his trigger finger gone, he would pose little trouble when Justice got around to dealing with him.

As soon as he caught up with Ashley.

Justice pulled up a hundred yards from the dead Indian pony, hot air rising from the blood that leaked onto the snow. Any other time, he would have simply followed to where Ashley's tracks led and killed him. But if Justice had learned anything about the man, he'd learned he was a survivor. He hadn't expected Ashley to have lived through the fierce blizzard wearing nothing else but his tattered clothes and a thin trade blanket. But when he saw Ashley disappear into the coulee atop the pony, he knew Ashley was still dangerous.

Justice dismounted and walked beside the gelding. He had shot the horse in the lower chest as it rode away. Like the Sioux who owned it, the pony was tough, and it had carried Ashley for another three miles before dying. Ashley's tracks leading due west showed he struggled to walk through the deep powder. That was all right, Justice thought—let him suffer a little more before I kill him.

He tried to remember what people had told him about the land ahead. The Lakota had lived in the Badlands as long as they had because the white man could not survive in the harsh terrain. If his recollection of a map was correct, Ashley was headed for the rim of the Badlands. A smart man would have left Indian country before another war party found him. But Ashley—frozen and his brain perhaps unable to process the danger—had ridden deeper into Sioux land for a reason. Hoping to run into more Lakota hell-bent on riding their land of white men? And they'd spot him riding while Ashley might be able to hide from them while they pursued Justice? That's what he would have done if someone pursued Justice who was tougher and meaner than Ashley. And possessed a horse and guns. And matches.

Something stuck out of the snow beside Ashley's tracks and fluttered. Justice thought at first it was a dead rabbit until he bent to it. A rabbit hide had been turned inside out. Blanket strips looped around it had torn loose, and the bottom of the hide was sliced through by sharp rocks. Ashley had managed to make it as far on foot as he had without his feet freezing because of the hides. "Amazing," Justice muttered to himself. "Almost makes me sorry to kill him. Almost."

A hundred yards farther along, Justice found the other rabbit hide, as ripped as the first, and he walked around Ashley's tracks to get a feel of what the man was thinking right now. He was on foot in freezing snow without even his rabbit-hide shoes. Even if he still retained some of the blanket he'd taken from the Indian, it would offer him little in the way of warmth. He was unarmed except for the Indian's knife. He also knew he was pursued by a man who—if Ashley had his wits about him and was whole physically—would have been more than his match. There was just no way Ashley could feel good right now.

As Justice mounted his horse, he followed the stumbling tracks of a dead man walking.

Chapter 35

Tucker rode the pony away from the ambush site as fast as the small horse could go in the deep snow. Only about twelve hands high, the small mare was struggling to break through the snow when a bullet hit it. Tucker fought to stay in the saddle, his legs and feet useless with numbing, his hands barely closing on the reins. The pony faltered with the blood loss, and it slowed to a stumble. But continued on.

Had Justice shot it? Tucker figured he probably had, as the Lakota would never shoot a fine pony, no matter who stole it. They might eat it if necessary—Tucker would, too, if he got the chance. The pony mirrored the Sioux—tough and struggling through, even at the end of life. In the end, Tucker had simply stepped off the horse as it lay down in the deep snow, unable to go farther, and died without complaint.

Another time, without Justice on his heels, Tucker would have skinned the pony. Fashioned shoes, which he desperately needed. Eaten the flanks. Perhaps climbed into the hot carcass to thaw himself. But Justice was no more than a couple of miles behind him, and Tucker had no time to butcher the horse. Or to hide his tracks.

If Tucker hadn't had his walking stick to keep him erect while he trekked, he might have fallen in the snow and never regained his footing. He stood little chance of defending himself when Justice found him. But he had made it to the rim of the Badlands, and now he had to find a spot to make his stand.

He peeked over the canyon rim at the edge of the Badlands. It dropped down a hundred feet. Perhaps two hundred. It was hard to tell, the snow having filled deep depressions in the Badlands bottom. He was walking along the edge for a hundred yards, looking over the side as he walked, his staff helping him from falling into the gaping mouth of the canyon when . . .

. . . he spotted a narrow trail that led down the face of the canyon. Tucker imagined mountain goats and sheep and pronghorns had used the trail for hundreds of years. And probably the Lakota, as well. It was one of the reasons they had never been beaten in this land—they went places the white man refused to go. Tucker was counting on Justice being as terrified as he was of traversing the game trail.

It took Tucker the better part of an hour to descend the thirty feet to a wide ledge along the goat trail. In good times—without bleeding, half-frozen feet and without shivering so violently that he knew death was mere hours away—he would have scrambled down in minutes. But he'd taken his time, carefully laid tracks he knew Justice could work out.

He *needed* Justice to follow him.

As he shivered from the terror of making his way down the canyon face, he leaned against the rock and caught his breath. He wrapped the ripped blanket tightly around his shoulder. But he *had* made it, and he stood on a stone ledge twenty feet across—wide enough for a man to build a fire and thaw out. If a man had a match.

He used the staff to probe the snow-covered rock face until he found what he wanted—an erosion in the side of the rock easily deep enough to hide a horse. Or a man pursued.

He turned back to the edge of the trail and looked down. A man falling would have no chance of survival. He was counting on that as he laid tracks up to the edge. He spread his blanket out over the snow and began backing away, brushing the snow off his footprints to conceal his tracks. He continued backing up to the depression he'd found, the blanket obliterating his tracks, aided by a wind that had come up within the last hour and begun covering the rock edge.

Satisfied Justice might not pick up on his tracks right off, Tucker backed up to the depression. He laid his staff with the knife lashed to the end so he could thrust it at Justice.

He shook snow off the blanket and wrapped it around his shoulders before he scooped snow all around him.

He sat immobile, and he grew even colder. Walking here, inching his way down the game trail, had brought circulation back to his legs and hands. But now, buried by the snow, and without moving, he felt his joints stiffen again. He prayed they would function when the time came.

And he knew that soon his ordeal would end.

One way or the other.

Chapter 36

Justice tied his horse to a rock before he walked to the edge of the canyon. He teetered as he looked down and backed away from the edge, rubbing his temples to ease his dizziness. Ashley's tracks clearly led down the narrow trail, though Justice couldn't imagine how the man had made it along the face of the canyon. He must be near-frozen, his legs barely working, but he had somehow accomplished the treacherous descent. Yet he had survived these last days when Justice thought he should have died. That knowledge drove him to make his way down the trail. Ashley ought to be dead now, and Justice could ride off and forget the frightening descent along the path.

But he *had* to see the body. He had come too far not to stand over Ashley's corpse and kick it for Elias and Gall and, yes, even for Henny. Inside, he hoped Ashley still lived. Justice wanted to look him in the eye and tell him the *real* reason he wanted him dead.

Even though it had become even colder these last hours, he took off his coat—the bulk would only hinder him, and it would take only a moment to verify the body. He left his hat hanging on the saddle horn and stepped to the edge. *Don't look down, fool,* he told himself as he took that first step. And the next, flattening himself against the rock wall. He looked down and froze. *Breathe. Look anywhere but down. Forget the fall . . .*

If Ashley himself hadn't fallen over the edge, Justice knew he might find the body frozen into some grotesque position, and for the briefest moment a twinge of regret crossed his mind. Ashley had killed his best friend and his brother. He had picked off Gall Manahan and caused untold agony in the days afterward, as Justice tracked him.

Still, the man had been a worthy enemy. He had not lain down and died when his fate appeared fruitless, like most of those Kansas farmers who refused to enter the conflict during the war. And he'd overcome odds that Justice thought he'd never survive. He would almost mourn the man's death. Almost.

Calmed down and concentrating on the rock face, Justice continued along the game trail. He followed Ashley's shuffling tracks until they reached a wide rock ledge. He leaned against the wall, grateful he would finally get his sea legs under him. He studied the tracks that led to the edge. He had so wanted Ashley to know the truth. But somewhere on the bottom of the canyon floor Tucker Ashley's body lay. Broken. Frozen by now when he had slipped and fallen the hundred feet.

He backed away from the ledge, and his legs buckled. He squatted and ran his fingers through hair pelted with snow.

Ashley was finally dead.

Justice had stood on shaky legs when something caught his eye, something that flapped against the face of the canyon.

A red and blue cloth like a trade blanket. Like the one Ashley took from the Indian. One corner stuck out of the snow. "What the hell . . . ?" He was bending to pick it up when . . .

The snow erupted off the rock face. Tucker Ashley burst from a mound of snow blown against the face of the canyon. He rushed at Justice as fast as a frozen man could rush and thrust the staff at him. Justice faltered for the briefest moment, and the knife at the end of the branch pierced his side. His legs buckled, and he regained his balance just as Ashley lost his hold on the staff. The oak branch skidded across the snow and plummeted over the edge.

He leapt the last few feet and clawed at Justice's throat. Justice lashed out, and the blow caught Ashley on the side of the head. He fell backwards, half buried in the snow.

Justice bled from the knife wound—a lung by the feel and sounds of it—and he turned to protect that injured side. He was yanking at his holster to get to his Colt when Ashley staggered to his feet and came at him again. His arms flailed the air. Justice easily stepped aside and threw a right cross that knocked Ashley to the ground. Blood dripped from a split lip, and his shattered eye socket had already started to swell. He managed to get an elbow beneath him to stand, but he fell back onto the ledge.

Justice drew his Colt and cocked it. He aimed it at Ashley's head, then de-cocked and holstered it.

"You have a change of heart?" Ashley spat blood and rubbed blood from his eye. "Or are you finally giving up?"

Justice smiled. "Y'all have a way of making me smile." He bent and hoisted Ashley to his feet. "You ever wonder why I want you to suffer so badly?"

" 'Cause you're a sadistic bastard."

Justice hit him on the face, and his nose shattered. Ashley slumped, and Justice hit him again. "You ever heard of Hellmira Prison Camp?" he asked when Ashley got to his knees.

"Where they send all sadistic bastards."

Justice hit him again, and a broken tooth flew from Ashley's mouth and landed in the snow beside him.

"Now y'all listen up, 'cause you don't have long left to learn the truth." Justice grabbed Ashley by his shirt and drew him close enough so that he could hear over the wind. "Because of you, I spent many a month fighting to survive in Hellmira."

Tucker tried wiggling free, but Justice was too strong. "You're not making any sense."

"1863. Little town across the Kansas border. Saloon connected to a Baptist church."

"I don't—"

"Quiet, while I finish." Justice slapped him. "I was there after a little . . . operation we had. A few farmers dead. A woman or two. But I was celebrating in that saloon when a Union patrol burst in and caught me while I was passed out behind the bar."

"So, you hate me because a Union patrol found you?"

Justice drew him close enough that Ashley could smell tea on his breath. "I hate you because *you* found me. It was you who tracked me there. And because of that, I was captured. Sent to Hellmira. Now you remember?"

"I recall tracking some Bushwhackers to a little Kansas town." Ashley nodded. "But I never went in." He tried focusing with his one good eye. "I was relieved of my mission before they stormed the saloon and sent back to my unit."

"So, you *do* remember?" Justice backhanded Ashley. Blood flew from his eye, mouth, and nose. "Now you know why—"

"And not because I killed your gang?"

"Let's just say that didn't help raise my opinion of you."

He hit Ashley in the mouth again, and he fell to the ground. Justice kicked him in the pit of the stomach, and the air rushed out of Ashley with a pitiful sound. "That was for Elias. Henny and Gall I could keep or toss aside. But the Norwegian . . ." He cocked his leg and lashed out again.

Ashley rolled away, and Justice stepped toward him. He kicked him again in the side, but, too late, he saw Ashley clutched a heavy rock in his hand. He swung it and connected with Justice's knee. The blow glanced off, but the leg buckled, and Justice drew his pistol.

Ashley smashed the rock down on Justice's hand.

The Colt flew from his grasp and skidded over the ledge into the canyon.

Justice snatched a belt knife and lashed out at Ashley's chest.

Blood quickly soaked Ashley's tattered shirt, and Justice stepped up to him to deliver the finishing thrust.

He knocked Ashley down and straddled him while he raised his arm.

Brought the blade down in a lethal arc, when . . .

. . . Ashley kicked Justice hard on the knee. He dropped the knife in the deep snow and staggered back. Ashley crawled toward him, and he elbowed Justice on the knee.

He howled in pain, clutching his leg. Staggered backwards.

Ashley stumbled, but managed to keep his balance. He stepped closer just as Justice swung a looping roundhouse. Even in Ashley's frozen state, he managed to duck, and Justice's fist glanced off Ashley's head.

Tucker's blow didn't.

He put all his might behind an overhand right. Justice jerked his head back—but too slow—and the blow caught him center chest.

He reeled, staggering back, fighting to keep his balance, when he stepped too close to the ledge.

One foot slipped.

He stumbled backwards when the other one slipped, and he slid over the ledge. One hand grabbed for a scrub tree growing out of the side of the rock ledge, and the other swiped the air for any handhold.

Ashley fell back onto the snow, heaving hard, coughing frothy blood that stained the ground. He looked through his one good eye at Justice dangling over the edge of eternity. "Help me, dammit," Justice pled.

Ashley started to speak, but he spat out another busted tooth. "Ain't that a bitch," he said as he focused on his tooth in his hand.

"Help me!" Justice said.

Ashley scooped snow up and rubbed his swollen eye. "Would

you help me? I don't think so."

Justice held his free hand upwards. "You got to help me." He looked down, and his face paled. "You *got* to give me your hand. You ride for the law."

Ashley shook his head. "No. All that means is I can't kill you slowly and painfully like you killed Velma. Like you killed the Swede's girl. Like you killed the posse that rode after you."

Justice tried pulling himself up, but his hand slipped on the icy ledge.

His other hand slipped on the tree, and he grabbed it with both.

Ashley gently brushed the snow out of his eye. "Don't mean I can't sit here and enjoy your predicament."

"Hurry," Justice said. "I can't hold on much longer."

Ashley scooted closer to the edge. "I'm not sure I have the strength—"

"Hurry."

Ashley reached down. "Give me your hand."

Justice looked down again and trembled, but he only looked at Ashley's outthrust hand. "How can I know you'll help me?"

"You said I ride for the law," Ashley said. "Now what lawman would let his prisoner fall to his death?"

Justice nodded, and Ashley grabbed his free hand.

Justice let loose of the tree.

Ashley let go of his hand, and Justice felt himself slip into eternity.

CHAPTER 37

Tucker looked over the edge of the canyon as Justice's screams became softer. Then they stopped entirely. Justice had careened off a rock outcropping before his broken body landed on the snowy bottom of the Badlands.

Tucker lay back on the ground and breathed in frigid air that seemed to pierce his lungs. His situation had changed little: he had no clothes. He had no weapon to protect himself from Indians who might come along any time. He had no food and no way to gather any. He was miles from any help, and he was physically worse off than he'd been since Justice had taken his boots and coat and weapons.

"You look like a damn mess."

Tucker stood painfully with a rock in his hand. He cocked his arm and turned to the threat.

Jack Worman carefully made his way down the game trail. A rope encircled his waist, and he wheezed heavily until he finally reached the wide ledge where Tucker stood. Jack grabbed him right before the adrenaline left him, and he slumped in Jack's arms. Jack led Tucker to the canyon wall and leaned him against it.

"You ought not be here," Tucker said. Jack's wheezing was loud, pronounced. "You got a punctured lung."

"Sounds like you got one, too," Jack said.

"Justice," Tucker said. "Caught me hard on the ribs. But I think they're just bruised."

"I figured that was him taking a dive into the canyon." Jack took the rope from his waist and looped it over Tucker's arms and shoulders. "I tried to get here sooner—"

"You were supposed to get to a sawbones."

Jack grinned. "I convinced Marshal Dawes I didn't have a punctured lung—I think all they are is cracked. Told him I was okay to ride."

"But you *aren't* okay." Tucker tapped Jack's side, and Jack drew in a sharp breath.

"I had to get away from the marshal. If I had to listen to that pompous ass one more day, I'd kill him myself. I convinced him I'd catch up with you while he rode for the nearest telegraph office."

"And right about now he's lunching with some banker or some fancy ladies and regaling them with his posse exploits."

"No doubt." Jack wrapped his arms around Tucker from behind. Jack grabbed onto the rope as they walked slowly up the game trail. When they reached the top, Jack untied the rope from his saddle horn and walked to Justice's black, tied a few yards away.

He grabbed Justice's coat and wrapped it around Tucker. "I can't do much for your feet, except put on some extra socks he has in his saddlebags. But at least you'll be able to ride his horse."

"He got any food in those bags?"

Jack shrugged. He rooted in Justice's bags.

And whistled. "Look what I found," he said as he held up a canvas bag. He hefted it, and coins clinked together. "Must be the money from all his jobs. You don't suppose we ought to . . ." Jack's voice trailed off.

Tucker forced a smile. "Now how far do you think we'd get before we turned ourselves in?"

Jack nodded. "Not far. We'll turn it over to the marshal when we get back to Ft. Pierre."

He replaced the bag and grabbed jerky Justice had stored in a leather pouch. Tucker wolfed two large pieces down before he felt it hit his gut. "Only thing we need now is a fire."

"My thinking," Jack said as he grabbed a match from his shirt pocket. "You relax for a bit while I get us some firewood."

Jack meandered away, grabbing pieces of sage and juniper branches that had blown onto the prairie, while Tucker lay back nibbling on another piece of jerky. Two friends alone. Who should not have survived what they had been through.

Tucker had no doubt that he would sleep well in the nights ahead, with Justice Cauther dead. Tucker had worked and fought with men who hated others. But Justice was special—hating a man who had tracked him to a saloon in a small Kansas saloon near ten years ago. Tucker had all but forgotten the incident. Justice never would have. Even if he'd killed Tucker, the hate would have festered in the man all his life.

He downed the last of the jerky and watched Jack build a fire. Jack struck the match to a branch, and the head broke off. "Careful with that!" Tucker said.

Jack fished in his vest pocket for another one. "It's just a match."

"It's never *just* a match," Tucker said.

CHAPTER 38

"What do I tell her folks?" Jack asked as he watched the steamer dock at Ft. Pierre. It had managed to break through the ice from Yankton, and Jack had worried himself sick these last few days after he heard it could make the passage. "I just don't know how to tell them about Velma."

Tucker clamped his hand over Jack's shoulder. "Tell them what you know—that she was killed during the robbery of the Bucket of Blood, and that's she's buried in a scenic spot out on the prairie. They don't need to know she was raped and tortured."

Jack turned his collar up against the icy wind blowing off the Missouri. "You're right. They don't need to know all that."

Tucker watched Jack walk to the boat when the plank was laid onto the dock. He didn't relish Jack's death message to Velma's folks. But right now, he had his own set of problems.

Tucker stopped short of entering the mercantile and backed away. He caught his reflection in the glass front: shabby clothes Jack had picked up in Hellion. Justice's coat that was a size too big. A pair of lace-up infantry boots he had taken from an army mount in front of the saloon in Hellion. It had taken him and Jack a week to ride back to Ft. Pierre, avoiding army patrols crisscrossing the prairie looking for Lakota that Tucker had no desire to run into.

The livery man in Hellion was mighty handy at doctoring

horses, and Tucker had to convince him he was equally adept at mending men. He had wrapped Tucker's ribs and sewed up the gash in his side where his stitches had broken. He had pasted a nasty-smelling poultice on his cheek to help heal the bones around his eye and had patched Jack's hand and his own ribs.

Tucker ran his fingers through his matted hair and looked at the Stetson in his hand. The brim had torn on the trail, and blood was embedded deep into it. He would need to buy a new one for the wedding. But at a shopkeeper's wages, it would take some time before he wore a new Boss.

He took a deep breath and entered the store. Tinkling bells announced him, and Miles Maynard looked up from behind a glass counter. "Well, look who finally came back." He arranged rounds of cheese, while Lorna wiped the glass display case with her apron. A large man reminding Tucker of a Union general he'd served under sat warming by the Franklin stove. He nibbled on crackers and a pickle as he glared at Tucker.

Lorna took off her apron and came around the counter. She smoothed her dress and pulled her hair from behind her ears. Maynard joined her and stood with his hand around her waist. "I see you've finally decided to come back."

Tucker had taken a step closer to Lorna when the large man stood and stepped between them. He was as tall as Tucker but had him by fifty pounds. Fifty soft pounds, and with the air of a man used to having his way. "So, *this* is Tucker Ashley."

Lorna nodded to the man. "My father, Tucker."

Tucker reached out his hand, but Everett Moore stood with his thumbs hooked in his suspenders. He looked Tucker up and down. "And you wanted to trade Miles for . . . this?"

"What's he mean, Lorna?"

"What Mr. Moore means," Maynard said, "is that Lorna got tired of waiting for you to drag yourself back to town."

"I don't understand—"

"Father explained how men like you are never happy settling down," Lorna began. "That the first chance you get to run free and leave your obligations behind—you do." She walked to the cracker barrel and took one out of the tin warming on the stove. She nibbled it daintily while she shook her head. "Like you did when you agreed to join the posse going after the Cauther gang."

Tucker felt his face and neck warm up more than it had in a week. "I went after them because they abducted Jack's girl. We can talk about this—"

"Too late," Everett said. "Show him."

Lorna held up her hand. A wedding band encircled her finger, and she hastily covered it with her other hand as if she were ashamed of it.

"You got married while I was away?"

"She did the only practical thing she could," Everett said, patting Maynard's shoulder. "She married someone stable. Someone able to stay with her. Give her a good life." He shook his head. "Not someone who goes around the world looking like a beggar." Everett took out his wallet and counted some bills. "This is for your inconvenience—"

"You buying me off?"

Everett shrugged. "Let us say it is your fee for rescuing Lorna from that renegade Sioux last summer."

"Keep your damned money," Tucker said.

The bells tinkled again, but Tucker ignored whoever entered. "Where I'm going, I won't need it."

Lorna scooted out from under Maynard's arm and stepped close to Tucker. "What will you need?" she almost pleaded, as if giving him something would ease her conscience. "Name it."

"All right, then," he pointed to a Sharps rifle hanging on the wall beside some new lever-action rifles. "I could use that."

Maynard laughed. "Not a Winchester, a buffalo gun? There's no buffalo hereabouts. But if that's what it will take to get you out of here . . ." He turned, took the rifle from the peg on the wall, and handed it to Tucker. "Might not be able to use it until you talk with those men."

"What men?"

Maynard nodded, and Tucker turned to see the men who had stepped into the mercantile. An army sergeant stepped up to Tucker and grabbed the Sharps from him. He handed it to the small, fat man standing behind him.

"We'll get this to you," Roush said. "After you've served your time."

Tucker had turned to Roush and grabbed his lapel when the sergeant and another NCO took hold of him from each side. He jerked away, but they held him tight as Roush produced a pair of shackles from under his tunic.

"What's going on here?" Tucker asked.

"Military justice," Roush said. "For beating a sergeant and stabbing the town marshal in Hellion. Not to mention setting some of my men afoot in winter and killing my best scout."

"Dilly is the one who came at me with his knives. And you sent your men after me in that saloon," Tucker said. "You ordered them to beat the hell out of me."

"I did no such thing." Roush turned to the sergeant. "Did you hear me order anyone to beat this man?"

The sergeant smiled. "No," he answered. "But by the time he gets released from the federal prison, he'll wish that's all we'd done to him."

When they dragged Tucker out of the mercantile, Maynard and Everett were grinning, but Lorna had a concerned scowl on her face. She was worried.

Tucker figured he ought to be, too.

AUTHOR'S NOTE

I chose to showcase the tracking abilities of my protagonist, Tucker Ashley, in this western series. Much has been speculated—brought about by movies and television dramas—about the tracking skills of western men. If one were to believe such stories, every man who lived in the frontier was competent in man tracking. This was certainly not the case. Diaries and personal accounts show how easily many folks in the west were deceived by their inability to read a track, or follow a simple trail. So, like today, men in the frontier that were track competent were in great demand. Where many lawmen could track across obvious terrain (snow, sandy creek beds, soft soil, etc.) the man who could age a track, or could decipher the number of riders on a particular horse, or any number of variables and anomalies associated with tracking was often sought out for his skills.

As a young Marine, I was first introduced to tracking while stationed in California, when border patrol agents from the Chula Vista office presented a class. I used those techniques they taught numerous times later as a law enforcement officer, where they often proved quite valuable. Although I did not intend for Tucker to be a teacher in the skills of tracking, the way in which he evaluates what he sees will be interesting to many folks.

ABOUT THE AUTHOR

C. M. Wendelboe entered the law enforcement profession when he was discharged from the Marines as the Vietnam War was winding down.

In the 1970s he worked in South Dakota. He moved to Gillette, Wyoming, and found his niche, where he remained a sheriff's deputy for over twenty-five years. In addition, he was a longtime firearms instructor at the local college and within the community.

During his thirty-eight-year career in law enforcement, he served successful stints as police chief, policy adviser, and other supervisory roles for several agencies. Yet he always has felt most proud of "working the street" in the Wild West. He was a patrol supervisor when he retired to pursue his true vocation as a fiction writer.

C. M. Wendelboe now lives and writes in Cheyenne, Wyoming.

The employees of Five Star Publishing hope you have enjoyed this book.

Our Five Star novels explore little-known chapters from America's history, stories told from unique perspectives that will entertain a broad range of readers.

Other Five Star books are available at your local library, bookstore, all major book distributors, and directly from Five Star/Gale.

Connect with Five Star Publishing

Visit us on Facebook:
https://www.facebook.com/FiveStarCengage

Email:
FiveStar@cengage.com

For information about titles and placing orders:
(800) 223-1244
gale.orders@cengage.com

To share your comments, write to us:
Five Star Publishing
Attn: Publisher
10 Water St., Suite 310
Waterville, ME 04901